James Williamson

An Argument for the Christian Religion

Drawn from a Comparison of Revelation

James Williamson

An Argument for the Christian Religion
Drawn from a Comparison of Revelation

ISBN/EAN: 9783337088361

Printed in Europe, USA, Canada, Australia, Japan

Cover: Foto ©Andreas Hilbeck / pixelio.de

More available books at **www.hansebooks.com**

A N

ARGUMENT

FOR THE

CHRISTIAN RELIGION;

DRAWN FROM A

COMPARISON of REVELATION

WITH THE

NATURAL OPERATIONS of the MIND:

Being the SUBSTANCE of

TWENTY-FOUR SERMONS

PREACH.ED AT

The LECTURE founded by the Hon. ROBERT
BOYLE, Efq; in the Parifh-Church of St. MARY-
LE-Bow, in the Years 1778, 1779, 1780,

IN FOUR BOOKS.

BY JAMES WILLIAMSON, B.D.

Bleffed are *the poor in fpirit: for theirs is the kingdom of
heaven.*

———————————

LONDON:
Printed for P. ELMSLY, in the Strand.
M.DCC.LXXXIII.

TO THE RIGHT HONOURABLE

Lord GEORGE CAVENDISH,

THE RIGHT HONOURABLE

Lord FREDERICK CAVENDISH,

THE RIGHT HONOURABLE

Lord JOHN CAVENDISH,

Trustees for the Lecture founded by the
Honourable Robert Boyle, Efq;

THIS DISCOURSE

IS MOST HUMBLY DEDICATED,

BY

THEIR LORDSHIPS

MOST OBLIGED,

AND MOST OBEDIENT,

HUMBLE SERVANT,

James Williamson.

AN
ARGUMENT

FOR THE

CHRISTIAN RELIGION.

BOOK I.

*Containing an Inquiry into the Rise and Pro-
gress of those Religious Opinions which seem
natural to all Mankind.*

CHAP. I.

Of PREJUDICE.

THE most remarkable circumstance in the
human character seems to be that great
uniformity of powers and inclinations which is
found among men; by which they are enabled to
act in concert, to extend their social union from
one extremity of the world to another, and to
join in any general effort to improve their nature
and faculties. Without this *sameness* of constitu-
tion there could have been no knowledge, for it
is this that enables one man to judge of the wants
and views of another, and of the probability of
his succeeding in any undertaking, almost with

the

the fame certainty as if the particular cafe had been his own; and thus alfo, our feelings being fimilar, we can fubftitute ourfelves in the place of another; and, by making his fchemes our own, partake of all his hopes and fears. And what is more, even our artificial habits,. as a confequence indeed of this, are nearly the fame; or if this is not naturally the cafe, from the great pliablenefs of the human mind, we have very little doubts of being able to make it fo : and our education muft be undertaken upon fuch a belief; for the very attempt to educate fuppofes that a man can form the fame habits in another which have been formed in himfelf. And thus the firmeft foundation feems to be laid for the greateft harmony of efforts and opinions among men. By exhibiting only one fide of human nature, a rational creature, who knew nothing of man but what he could learn from that view, ought to be convinced that there never could be fuch a thing as a difpute in the world; nothing but wifdom and ignorance liftening and inftructing each other.

Yet notwithftanding this general uniformity of character and abilities difcoverable in the human fpecies ; it is no lefs true that, in many refpects, the faculties and inclinations of men are extremely different, indicating, whenever occafions offer, ftrong inclinations to different purfuits, from the earlieft infancy. And although mankind are all formed with the fame faculties, and fhould happen to have the fame feeds of inftruction fown in their minds, yet they will neglect fome and cultivate others without any reafon of preference, apparent to themfelves or others; and this will produce many different opinions and views of things, which, we fay, very properly, fpring from prejudice.

I   Nor

Nor is this any blemish in our conftitution, when it is confidered, that we are in a ftate, where much of our improvement is left to ourfelves. And the attentive obferver will accordingly find, that much of the bufinefs, and much of the improvement of the world, has no other fpring to put it in motion, but prejudices of one kind or another. A genius, bent or inclination for particular employments, arts or purfuits; the prejudice of rank, profeffion and education, to fay nothing of national prejudice, are fuch powerful inftruments in human affairs, that the actions of mankind would be deprived of the great principle which governs them and keeps them in vigour, if thefe prejudices made no part of our conftitution. In fhort, we are formed with fuch a variety of talents and difpofitions; feemingly on purpofe to teach us, that by the very nature and 'adjuftment of the feveral parts of our conftitution, we are predetermined, and as it were, formed for certain purpofes; and that it never was the intention of our Creator, in our prefent imperfect ftate, to have all mankind of the fame opinion; but that the rich and the poor; the foolifh and the wife; the active and the indolent, fhould misjudge, defpife and envy each other's fituation, attainments, and circumftances. For, with the ordinary infirmities of human nature, and deprived of the advantages arifing from prejudices of different kinds, man, in all probability, would have been a ftupid, fplenetic, fenfual and unteachable animal; as the improvement both of the individual and of the fpecies, according to the prefent ftate of the world, feems chiefly to be carried on by jarring principles and falfe or inadequate profpects of things: And human frailty makes this almoft the fureft way to

truth,

truth, fo little are we influenced by the naked reality of things.

It is upon this ground that it might be faid, that much mifchief may be done, by endeavouring haftily and injudicioufly to remove real prejudices. For, it is extremely probable that, inftead of fub-ftituting truth in the place of them, we are only exchanging one prejudice for another: and the confequence may be much worfe, if nothing be fubftituted in their room, becaufe thus all our principles of action may be deftroyed; and many, whofe worldly circumftances place them at their eafe, have their principles of action, in reality, thus deftroyed. For when you have once con-vinced a man, in a few inftances, that what he took to be a ferious and well-founded truth is only prejudice, there will be very little difficulty in perfuading him to rank a troublefome truth among prejudices. Tell a rich man that Religion is nothing but prieftcraft; that patriotifm is a farce; and that he himfelf is a fool, if he do not enjoy his wealth, in every way which his appetites prompt him, and, if your opinion has any weight or credit with him, he will foon lofe fight of every duty, and forget that he himfelf is fupported by fociety, finking gradually into a fenfual creature, until he becomes (as the fcripture very emphati-cally expreffes the ftate of the Antediluvians) *nothing but flefh.*

And yet furely prejudices ought to be removed, though not in the fuperficial manner practifed by modern reformers. The reafoning of ages, cor-rected and fupported by a frequently varied ex-perience, is neceffary for giving a firm eftablifh-ment to fome truths, efpecially fuch as have had a general prejudice againft them: As, on the other hand,

hand, thofe truths, which are a check upon the paffions of men, will be readily turned over to the clafs of prejudices, upon the ftrength of a joke, or of the moft fanciful and ill-founded reafonings : and therefore every wife, or even prudent, man will reject thofe abfurd or at beft inadequate methods of levelling prejudices, however fafhionable, which are borrowed from theoretical fpeculations, ornamented, but not fupported, by facts; and propofed to the world in this form chiefly, becaufe they are fuppofed to fall in with the humour of the times, which, at prefent, is by no means that of fearching whether the things propofed to our confideration have a firm foundation in experience, or depend upon well-attefted facts.

Truths ought to be examined by the nature and circumftances of men and things, and not according to the limited, fanciful and partial notions of true and falfe, in the eftablifhing of which mankind feem to have difcovered a more than ordinary degree of folly, at the very time when they are producing themfelves as models of wifdom, and ftandards for regulating the judgement of the whole world. Mankind have a certain fphere allotted them, within which they may act with propriety and judge with certainty, but when they attempt excurfions beyond this, they bring nothing back but proofs of their vanity and folly.

Nor is this without its ufe, when it is confidered, that it is only by comparifon that we can regulate or change our opinions : and therefore right and wrong, truth and falfhood, wifdom and folly muft be plentifully fown over the world, merely as the neceffary means of improvement to rational and limited creatures, in all thofe circumftances, where

B 3 their

their conduct and opinions are to depend upon themfelves, acting as free agents, and without fupernatural inftruction. And if our errors were merely of a fpeculative nature, implying only greater or lefs degrees of wifdom or folly, time and chance, or the feveral accidents of the world, would go a great way towards correcting them.

But our weak fide is where our morals are concerned; and it is here that, in a particular manner, we are apt to delude ourfelves, and are expofed to the attacks of delufion. It is true God has particularly guarded us from fuch errors, by ftrong natural fentiments, in favour of virtue; but, in an improved ftate of fociety, our duties multiply upon us, and become more difficult to perform, from the increafe of temptations; and finding them burthenfome, we are eafily difpofed to liften to any reafons for neglecting them. Yet, if the fact were not certain, it would feem very extraordinary that Reafon and Religion fhould have often been employed to furnifh arguments for fuch a neglect, and to eradicate the natural fentiments, implanted in the mind by God himfelf.

It is undoubtedly true, that our morals may be corrupted or improved, by human reafon and Religion: they are both dangerous inftruments, when in improper hands, becaufe in their natural and original ftate, as formed by men to fupply their moft preffing neceffities, they are little better than the blundering operations of ignorance, paffion and prejudice; and confequently are more dangerous than thefe, being a compofition made out of them veiled with a kind of authority; and may do good or harm according as they are employed to counteract or fupport the failings and imperfections of mankind.

Not

Not that I confider both as equally in the power of men to regulate. The circumftances of the world continually improve or corrupt the reafon of men, fo that it can hardly ever be ftationary, except where human nature is degraded almoft below the rational level, while their religious opinions never vary from their original abfurdity. And had there never been a real revelation, I queftion whether there ever had been fuch a thing as a religious difpute in the world, in the fenfe in which that word is underftood among Chriftians. Men would have changed their religious opinions, with as little difficulty, and even with as little confequence, as they do the fafhion of their cloaths. And thus it happens that by their rational exertions alone, we can trace the progrefs, refinement and corruptions of nations; but even where mankind have exhibited the greateft variety of extraordinary abilities, we find their Religion during all thefe changes the fame inanimate mafs of corruption as we found it at the beginning.

I faid the circumftances of the world improve, but I think they are even fufficient for perfecting human reafon, though a deliberate and extenfive obfervation is neceffary for this purpofe, inftead of the hafty way of voting every thing a prejudice, which does not agree with the mode of thinking which may be in fafhion at the time. Many truths are relative, and fuited to particular circumftances; and if the circumftances be changed, thefe truths muft vary with them. They may be relative to our fenfations: Thus the fame water may convey, the different and even oppofite fenfations of heat and cold, to the fame perfon at the fame time: and bodies at reft may appear to be

in

in motion or the contrary. Truths of this kind partake of the nature of prejudice, and are only to be affented to, when referred to a particular ftandard. A ftandard derived from the nature of heat, or the nature of motion, would be more accurate than our fenfes: and yet no man, with impunity, can neglect his fenfations; and he would lofe too much by having his body converted into a thermometer.

There are truths alfo which have the human faculties for their ftandard, which muft be very variable, as they will depend upon that view of the fubject, which different people may take, which will be as various as their faculties and improvements; and yet all fuch are truths in a certain fenfe, and are by no means to be neglected; it is only neceffary to know the true nature of fuch truths, fo as to be able to refer them to their proper clafs. We have likewife artificial truths which mankind have made fuch arbitrarily, and in many of them feem to have confulted nothing but their own humour. Thofe who would confine truth to mathematical demonftration, do not confider that human nature cannot afford that all the world fhould be mathematicians, with their views confined folely to the properties of extenfion and number.

Yet, amidft fuch a chaos of opinions and prejudices, it is poffible to arrive at a confiftency in thinking; for the natural progrefs of fociety cures fuch prejudices, or rather fhews them in their proper light, and more perfect notions of things are the confequence of every improvement, which is generally grounded upon a more accurate and extenfive experience, founded however upon the firft imperfect notions, fo that a progrefs through
them

them ſeems to be neceſſary: for I am certain that a man who never had any prejudices, never had, nor can have any real knowledge. And thus by attention mankind may, in proper circumſtances, gradually ſhake off their prejudices, and gain ground upon every ſubject which reaſon can improve; either making their notions more accurate or their views more extenſive, arriving at what might be called the perfection of reaſon. In ſhort this ſeems to be a talent, with the improvement of which mankind may be ſafely entruſted, nor ought they in this caſe to look for ſupernatural aſſiſtance.

It is very different however with Religion; for the prejudices ariſing from ſuperſtition ſeem beyond the power of man to correct, and the taſk ſeems to have been put into his hands for no other purpoſe but to convince him of his inability. Of all our natural propenſities the call to be religious, both from our faculties and circumſtances, appears to be the ſtrongeſt; and thus it comes to paſs, that the haſty notions which we are obliged to take up with at firſt, are but little in our power to regulate afterwards, being chiefly ſuggeſted by the imagination, prompted by fear, which creates prejudices of a very different kind from thoſe, which have their firſt beginnings in the imperfection of our ſenſes. The improvements of ſociety may give our religious notions a faſhion, or be the occaſion of adding or taking away ſomething; which it is eaſy to do without ſkill or without producing any improvement, when you have a confuſed maſs to work upon: It may change its ſize or ſhape without gaining or loſing any thing in proportion, utility or beauty, there being no ſtandard to which it can be referred.

The

The prejudices of fenfe are founded in facts, and may be corrected by facts, but the prejudices of fuperftition are founded in the imagination, and can only be changed for new fancies equally extravagant and groundlefs as the former, and this never could produce any improvement. And thus it happened that the heathen fuperftitions were become a monfter which was to be crufhed and annihilated by an irrefiftible power, as being irreducible to any confiftent or rational fhape; and the memory of it only preferved as a proof of human weaknefs and extravagance.

And to fupply its place the Chriftian Religion prefents itfelf to us, though in a very different manner. It produces itfelf as a fixed truth, an unalterable and determinate matter of fact, to which nothing can be added, and from which nothing can be taken away by men; demanding credit, and, at the fame time, profeffing itfelf to be above human comprehenfion; difdaining to be tried by any teft of human invention, but, forcing a new kind of evidence upon us, the evidence of faith; which hurts our philofophic pride, and creates it great oppofition from the wife men of this world, who think that every fubject is to be new modelled to advantage by their faculties. And this Religion, refufing to accommodate itfelf to circumftances, by favouring the vices and views of mankind, breeds no lefs enmity againft itfelf among the worldly-minded, whofe paffions and wifhes are generally at variance with its doctrines.

This is a yoke that mankind never could have laid upon their own necks, and therefore muft owe its beginning, progrefs, and fupport to fome foreign caufe: and what that caufe may be is an inquiry of more importance to us than any thing whatever.

Superftition

Superstition and a true Religion are equally unmanageable by reason. Nevertheless human reason is very capable of examining their different characters, even so accurately that a man may chuse with certainty between them. And as we have no direct standard of revelation in our minds to appeal to, a comparison of the Christian Religion with the superstitions natural to men, and the operations of the human understanding, seems to be the most general and rational ground of conviction upon this subject, at least it is almost the only effectual method for removing all religious prejudices, which equally enslave the Christian and the philosopher. And for this purpose, I propose to lay before you, what I take to be the natural operations of the human mind, under the dominion of passion and the guidance of reason, upon the subject of Religion : and, by shewing what a different system would be produced, prove that the Christian Religion comes from God.

But here there are a class of prejudices which stand in our way, very different from those already mentioned, as they are not marks of weakness of understanding, but of the strength of passion. A prejudice against a person, a prejudice against a subject, and others of the like kind. *Is not this the carpenter's son ? These are hard sayings, who can hear them?* Such prejudices when they are without malice, and taken up merely as a pretence to indulge an indolent disposition or to remove a disagreeable truth out of sight, are far from being innocent. A man's ears should always be open to conviction, and our attention should be more especially roused to disagreeable truths. Even he who thinks he has reason to wish wifh that the contents of the Bible may not be true, ought not to let his wifhes, fo far get the better of his underftanding, as to neglect attending to the evidence offered to his confideration, and implicitly believe thofe, who tell him that there is no difference between Chriftianity and the fuper-ftitions of the heathens. A man who fuffers him-felf to be deluded into fuch an opinion, upon the partial reprefentation of a few detached facts, is exactly in the fituation of one who could be led to defpife the moft excellent compofition of human genius, by having it reprefented to him, that all the words in it were to be found in the dictionary; only with this difference, that the one would be the fubject of human ridicule, but the other of divine vengeance.

C H A P. II.

Of the Nature and extent of Superftition, as de-rived from the Faculties and Circumftances of Men.

SUPPOSE mankind left to difperfe themfelves in this world, with fuch faculties as we find them poffeffed of at prefent, and under the do-minion of their ordinary paffions; making their way through dangers and temptations, without any other aid or impediment than what they may receive from one another; and in this fituation, we know that they would foon be fenfible of many wants, and liable to many apprehenfions, and much the greateft number of thofe impoffible to be relieved or removed by any of the objects which prefented themfelves. Nay, whoever fhould hap-

pen

pen to be ſo much maſter of circumſtances, as to be able to chuſe any particular ſituation, even the moſt favourable to health and happineſs which this world affords; and together with this could place himſelf in the moſt diſtinguiſhed rank in life; if he promiſed himſelf compleat happineſs even from theſe ſingular privileges, he would find by experience that he was but little ' acquainted with himſelf. Becauſe it appears from the paſſions implanted in human nature, that man, inſtead of being formed to have his views fixed upon any determinate ſet of objects, is intended for various ſtages and ſtates of exiſtence; and not like the beaſts to have his wiſhes confined to the preſent moment. And although every climate, every age, every rank in life furniſh certain enjoyments and gratifications; yet no climate, no period of time, no rank or ſtation in life can fully gratify all his affections and deſires, and ſecure him againſt the accidents of futurity; his ſatisfactions alſo ariſing more from his future proſpects than from any preſent enjoyments. And therefore a man will depend upon the future, more than upon any thing which he poſſeſſes for the preſent; and the things of futurity being contingent, and even the preſent uncertain, eſpecially in the early periods of ſociety; hopes and fears will engage moſt of his attention; for it is only by theſe that uncertain things and the things of futurity are to be eſtimated.

In the early period, of which I am now ſpeaking, mankind would have no experience to direct them; they could learn no leſſon from the hiſtory of the ſucceſs or failures of others; and from a conſciouſneſs of their own weakneſſes, with the help of a few diſappointments, no ſcheme that they could devife would appear after a little experience, by any means certain to bring about the ends they might have in view. I fay after a little expe- rience, becaufe, before mankind had any fettled rules or plans to direct them, they would be con- tinually blundering, even in their moft ordinary bufinefs, which would very much weaken any na- tural confidence which they might have in them- felves, to a degree that when they happened to fucceed, the accomplifhment of their fchemes would be referred to fomething befides their own ingenuity. And very flight things indeed will have fome influence in a ftate of fufpence and uncertainty, for a throw of the dice, coinciding with a man's own wifhes, will give him fome fpirits, and even determine him to act, fo naturally have we recourfe to fecret and unfeen influence ; and that degree of prudence, which is to deprive Fortune of her rank as a divinity, could not be reached by the Romans in their higheft ftate of improvement, which is owned by Juvenal in thefe lines :

> Nullum numen habes, fi fit prudentia : fed te
> Nos facimus, Fortuna, Deam, cœloque locamus.

We who have the laws of nature and the prin- ciples of Religion reduced to a kind of certainty, which in fome fenfe makes us independent, can hard- ly conceive the perplexity and anxiety of mankind in a ftate of nature, or during the firft beginnings of fociety, efpecially when agitated by thofe hopes and fears, which are raifed by the certainty of death, and the uncertainty of the time when it will happen. Now, upon trying occafions, where a man's own powers and all the natural means which his reafon can fuggeft have been exhaufted,

where

where is he to look for aſſiſtance? Certainly it
ſeems natural that a man in real or imaginary
diſtreſs, after he has done his beſt in a natural
way, will ſet his own imagination or that of others
to work, in order to form ſome *Being* with ſuch
powers and attributes as his particular circumſtances require, and his immediate wants ſtand in
need of. I have mentioned the imagination of
others, becauſe there is ſome reaſon to think, that
the imaginations of his neighbours would be chiefly
employed in this god-making buſineſs; for a man
in dread or danger rejects no advice that is offered
him, and has a better opinion of every body's underſtanding than of his own. His neighbour might
recommend it to him, to do any thing in jeſt or
earneſt; and as things are often apprehended to
be worſe than they turn out to be, the ſuperſtitious man aſcribes it to ſome inviſible interpoſition, that his misfortunes did not come up to the
meaſure of his own fears.

But ſuch *Beings* cannot anſwer the ſuperſtitious
man's purpoſes without a will and a kind of free
agency, ſuperadded to a power of producing effects; and as ſuch a *Being* cannot be compelled,
he muſt be entreated to lend his aſſiſtance, or
perhaps bribed to do it, ſo much are men diſpoſed
to make their Gods after their own image: Becauſe
this cannot be ſuch a power as produces effects by
the application of one material agent to another,
in ſuch a manner that its aſſiſtance may be regularly expected whenever certain means have been
uſed. For the diſcovery of ſuch powers is not the
work of the imagination, but the effect of a regular and attentive experience.

Now, a ſupernatural Being endued with free
agency will never ſubmit his actions to the teſt of
experience;

experience; and this very circumftance carries fuch delufions beyond the reach of experience to remedy. For after a thoufand failures and difappointments, the fuperftitious man will ftill continue to vary the mode of his application, with a conftant and firm perfuafion that there is a remedy fomewhere, although he has not been fo lucky as to find it.

His Deity, that he applied to, may want inclination or perhaps power from the bufinefs being out of his province: he will therefore have recourfe to fome other Gods; and will furnifh himfelf with an excufe for every difappointment; and the large clafs of feemingly contingent events, will feed his hopes, alarm his fears, and keep up his delufions.

And thus it comes to pafs that no rational creature can enjoy life, or even fupport it, without religious opinions of one kind or another: if a Religion be not communicated to him, he will make one for himfelf which muft ferve him for a temporary relief, though it fhould happen not to be of that determinate or durable kind which his circumftances may require. For even the unbeliever himfelf will readily acknowledge that he was in fome part of his life a fuperftitious creature; and that the triumph over fuperftition was only the laft effort of his rational faculties.

To fuppofe a people without Religion feems to me the fame thing as to fuppofe a people without hopes and fears; for it is impoffible to gratify and keep up thofe paffions, but by fuch objects as will lead men beyond their own natural abilities, even to fuch a degree as to make them put their truft in any thing fooner than relinquifh all hopes.

It

It is true, the religious principle taken in this fenfe is very general, and may be gratified and fupported by any thing whofe powers we are not acquainted with. Any thing animate, or inanimate, real or imaginary to which credulity or knavery has afcribed any fupernatural or extraordinary powers, may be the object of fuperftition; and the lefs we are acquainted with the nature of things, the fitter will they be, for being turned to fuperftitious ufes. For this and other obvious reafons the heavenly bodies are moft likely to challenge the attention of a fuperftitious man; and as life would appear to him an advantage, he would likewife fuppofe the ftars endued with life and fpontaneous motion, which would be readily believed of *Beings* fo far beyond the reach of vulgar knowledge.

Nor would mankind be content with gods fimply to protect them; but they would require others to affift them in the gratifications of their paffions, in fhort as this kind of fupernatural affiftance could be fo eafily had, they would not be very fcrupulous in having recourfe to it, upon almoft every occafion.

This reprefentation, it is true, defcribes mankind as given over to delufion, from the very nature of their faculties, paffions and affections; and that to fuch a degree, as would overpower their reafon, corrupt their morals, and prevent all improvement, unlefs fome circumftances fhould concur to moderate or correct this infatuation.

C

CHAP.

C H A P. III.

Of the natural Remedies of Superstition.

BUT it is to be observed that all our hopes and fears cannot be immediately grounded on Religion. Mankind would find that some wishes were to be gratified even fully, by a proper use of their natural faculties, and by the application of one material agent to another; and that some evils were to be avoided by the same means, in a more regular and effectual manner than by any mode of superstition.

This discovery, it might be pretended, would be the occasion of a division of events into such as were in our own power, and such as exceeded it; and that the province of superstition would thus come to be marked out, though by very arbitrary limits; as mankind might rather be said to have found out a rule for settling it, than to be possessed of sufficient means or materials, to ascertain the proper bounds : having recourse to superstitious practices when they ought to use their own natural powers; or joining the superstitious practices to the exertions of their natural powers, they would allow the superstition a large share of the merit of the success. And though this would retard the progress of their improvement at first, yet taking it once for granted that they could do something of themselves, it might be said, that the more they improved their faculties, the dominion of superstition would be proportionably lessened, and why not in time compleatly abolished.

But

But thoſe who reaſon in this manner ſeem to forget that ſuch reformers have no materials to work with, at leaſt none fit for ſuch an under-taking. Their building would become a caſtle in the air, which the leaſt blaſt of the boiſterous paſſions would demoliſh. The truth of this aſ-ſertion will be beſt determined by tracing the pro-greſs of ſuperſtition, and by conſidering the addi-tions and impediments which it is likely to receive from the circumſtances of men and things.

Thoſe who have proper notions of the power of a ſtock or a ſtone, even when dignified with the honour of being the repreſentative of an imagi-nary ſupernatural *Being*, will readily believe that ſuch as put their truſt in them would be frequently diſappointed. Yet, when they had once gone ſo far as to honour them as gods, inſtead of aſcribing the failure to the true cauſe, they would naturally conclude that the diſappointment originated from ſomething in themſelves; ſo much do mankind work in the dark, when they work with ſuper-ſtition. They would ſuppoſe that they had been deficient in reſpect to this ſupernatural *Being*, or were ignorant of the proper way of approaching him, ſo as to render him propitious. Cunning men, and perhaps cunning women, would take advantage of this diſpoſition of the people, and making pretences that they were in the ſecret, or perhaps fancying themſelves to be ſo, would turn the credulous humour of the multitude to their own advantage, by ſetting up the trade of con-ſulting oracles, and influencing ſupernatural powers.

Nor would it be long before ſuch inſtances of great weakneſs would be daily preſented to them, as could not fail to lead them to conceive a very

C 2   high

. high opinion of the credulity of mankind, though a more contemptible one of their understanding than they had before. For inftead of requiring art to deceive the multitude, they would find every hour furnifhing them with dupes, prefenting themfelves, and tempting them to deceive them from the eafinefs of the undertaking, or rather who would go more than half way to deceive themfelves.

A man's natural fuperftition is a very heavy load, which he would be very glad to transfer fomewhere elfe with the firft opportunity: and thus any kind of public creed, would be fuch a relief, of which he could not fail to take the firft advantage. For though the pride of man, when he is entirely at his eafe, is continually lifting him up to independence, yet when he is allowed to feel his real fituation, he is glad to be directed, and is fond of living in a crowd profeffing the fame fentiments with himfelf, either from a fenfe of weaknefs, or an averfion to trouble.

Nothing therefore could be more agreeable to any one in fuch circumftances, than to have his fuperftition fo well regulated, that he had only to repair to a certain place, and do as he was inftructed, or as he faw others do; which would keep his mind at eafe, and flatter his indolence.

Nor would the philofophic fpirit, prevailing in a Nation, be able to give any check to fuperftition. For philofophy requires an adequate caufe to produce an effect, and fuch as will always produce the fame effect, and neither one greater or lefs; whereas, according to the fuperftitious man, a few words may bring down the Moon: *Carmina vel cælo poffunt deducere Lunam*; which is fufficient to fhew the abfurdity of attempting to overcome

by

by any fixed rules, a prejudice which diſdains all rule.

But I ſhould be glad to know how the philoſophers themſelves, were to eſcape the general infection : that they did not is an undoubted fact; for the moſt ancient philoſophers had their reaſonings about natural things ſtrongly tinctured with ſuperſtition, and were no leſs abſurd in the cauſes which they aſſigned, than the moſt ſuperſtitious of the vulgar. What ſhall we ſay of Cleanthes's opinion as handed down by Cicero, which ſhews his underſtanding to have been ſo perverted, that it is not eaſy to conceive by what ſteps it could have been rectified. "Ali autem "Solem, Lunam, reliqua aſtra, aquis alia dul- "cibus, alia marinis. Eamque cauſam Cleanthes "affert, cur ſe ſol referat, nec longius progre- "diatur ſolſtitiali orbe, itemque brumali, ne lon- "gius diſcedat a cibo." Thus we find according to this philoſopher (whoſe opinions, abſurd as they are, antiquity thought worth the preſerving) the ſun is a free agent, and like an animal goes to the different ſides of the equator in ſearch of food. Surely ſuch philoſophers were much more likely to increaſe than to diminiſh the ſtock of vulgar ſuperſtitions.

If it ſhould be ſaid that ſuch a philoſophy as Newton's might cure mankind of the greateſt part of their ſuperſtitions, as it would at leaſt give them true and proper notions of that *hoſt of heaven*, which was ſo general an object of their ſuperſtition. But it ſeems impoſſible to conceive that ſuch ſpeculations would have been tolerated or reliſhed, or even thought of, among a people addicted to the ſuperſtition of regarding the heavenly bodies as divinities.

C 3 And

And if a philosopher had been possessed of such a discovery, he never durst have published it; for certain death would have been the consequence of such a daring and impious thought, as the reducing such glorious bodies, to the same condition as the dirt and rubbish which we trample under our feet. Such powerful patrons are the people of the idols which they set up, whether gods or men. They feel their own weakness to such a degree, as will not suffer them to allow the least inquiry into the nature and qualities of their Idols.

However, let us suppose such a discovery made and published to the world; I think it would in this case have no effect; because one thing is certain, that the true knowledge even of those general laws which take place in the solar system, must always, as it is at present, be confined to a very few, not taking in at a moderate computation the thousandth part of those that are generally reputed learned; and therefore could never banish from the world the notions of planetary influence, and other superstitions depending upon the stars. And if it had not been for the Christian Religion, instead of making use of Eclipses for settling the longitude of places, we should have still been beating drums to relieve the Moon in labour.

This glimmering of light, which had to pass through the dark medium of intricate computation, would soon have been extinguished and overpowered by the clouds that would have been raised to intercept it.

The sophistical reasonings of such as might happen to have a command of language, and a turn of argument suited to the humour of mankind, would have soon got the better of every thing that could have been alledged in favour of

such

such a system. Tradition, a flight of the imagination, and a certain fanciful art of representing things by similitudes, would make their way very readily to such heads, as shew themselves but ill disposed to follow the steps of a mathematical demonstration. This discovery made its way but slowly, and with difficulty, in an age when mankind seemed to be panting after that kind of knowledge: such a discovery, therefore, in the dark ages of superstition would have vanished, leaving human nature at liberty to resume all its antient superstitions. And even from a view of what at present is called natural philosophy, I see great reason to apprehend that Newton's discoveries will become traditionary tales; the preserving and communicating the principles of them requiring a greater expence of thought than the present age can afford to bestow.

It has also been said that politicians invented Religion; and of course, when they pleased, might have destroyed their own inventions, and extirpated superstition, by letting the world into the secret of the imposition that had been put upon them. It would be just as wise and reasonable to say that they invented hunger and thirst, or any other natural appetites, for all these are equally the gift of nature, and have been, upon occasion, converted by politicians to answer their purposes. They have been *often* able to regulate the modes of gratifying the appetites of hunger and thirst, and legislators have *sometimes* modified superstition, in order to make it, as far as they could, consistent with the good of society; and the little morality, that is sometimes discoverable in the heathen Religion, is probably their work: For a man of himself would never have recourse to supernatural as-

C 4 sistance

fistance for the regulation of his morals, this being a want that individuals never feel.

But the misfortune is, that legislators and philosophers had no standard for directing themselves in their alterations, had they been never so well disposed, but the good of society, which they all conceived to be consistent with a multitude of the worst kinds of superstition. A legislator might be able, so far to lay the man aside, while he was considering any scheme of policy, as to keep his own weaknesses out of sight; but he had neither knowledge nor authority to go any farther than to modify the superstitions.

If the people were disposed to claim a general indulgence of certain passions, from the example of their gods, the magistrate might so far prevail, as to persuade them that this indulgence was to be confined to a certain time and place, and perhaps carried on in the form of a religious ceremony.

Even if the supreme magistrate had the power of destroying certain superstitions for a time, as he had not the ability to put any thing more rational in their place; a superstition so checked would only undergo a temporary cessation, and after a little while human nature would be the same as before. Thus we find legislators and philosophers attempting to act a part for which they were by no means qualified.

Nor does any thing that they have either said or done, in the least convince me, that they were not themselves extremely superstitious. If he had not told us so himself, one could have hardly been brought to believe, that Lord Herbert, the father of the Deists, and the great reasoning champion that was to destroy the Christian superstition, was a firm believer in the *animation* of the stars: and
though

though too acute a reaſoner to be fit to be a diſ-
ciple of Chriſt, would have made a figure as one
of Cleanthes's. And this was his opinion in the
only philoſophical age that the world has ever ſeen.
So unfair is it to form a judgment of the entire
ſtate of the human mind, by a ſolitary ray of reaſon
iſſuing from it.

A man by accident may have fallen into ſome
lucky train of thought, which might produce
ſpeculations that would raiſe him not only above
the vulgar, but even above himſelf; and make it
become a point of honour with him to keep himſelf as much as poſſible above the weakneſſes of
common men. But when this becomes impracti-
cable, the character muſt be ſupported by diſ-
ſimulation; and it is only in unguarded, or very
trying moments, that we loſe ſight of the philoſopher and diſcover the man; at leaſt he acts his
part but indifferently, if he diſcover himſelf in his
writings. Socrates ſacrifices a cock to Eſculapius,
and by ſo doing proves himſelf to be as ſuperſtitious as the vulgar.

We go to conſult the antient philoſophers,
with the ſame diſpoſition and turn of mind, that
the vulgar go to a conjurer : we wiſh to find them
of the ſame opinion that we ourſelves have adopted
or wiſh to eſtabliſh ; and thus contrive to make
them deliver us back our own knowledge, and
then wonder how they became acquainted with it;
concluding that little obſcure hints, which we
force a meaning upon, that never entered into
the heads of the authors, ought to have reformed
the whole human race. The pagan philoſophers
are made to write good morality, and a rational
natural Religion, by the ſame art that Auſonius
makes Virgil write obſcenity.

The

The Chriſtian Religion has ſomething grand in the very manner that it ſets about reforming the world; it makes the attack upon the great maſs of the people, who began, ſupported, and ſpread the deluſions of ſuperſtition, and who were entirely out of the reach of philoſophic improvement.

The more this ſubjeƈt is examined, the more it will be found, that neither philoſophy, nor any kind of human learning could do any thing towards correƈting or extirpating the vulgar ſuperſtitions, as they could ſubſtitute nothing in the room of the ſuperſtition to ſupply its place in the mind. The deteƈtion of religious impoſitions ſeems to be the only thing likely to ſtop the progreſs of ſuperſtition. Such diſcoveries, if very frequent, would run the half-thinkers, and ſuch as had received ſtrong provocation from impoſters, into a kind of occaſional atheiſm. And many people of abandoned principles would be glad to creep under ſuch a ſhelter, where they might indulge their paſſions without controul. But ſober men, and ſuch as took pains to weigh conſequences, would ſee that ſuch inferences were the effeƈts of paſſion, and not of argument; or that what argument there was, did by no means conclude againſt religious opinions in general; for they would find that it proved nothing in faƈt, but that one man would cheat another when he had it in his power: and when the prejudices thus raiſed were worn away, the ſame opinions would again prevail as powerfully and extenſively as before.

Even thoſe who made objeƈtions to the moſt trifling ſuperſtitions, might expeƈt to be anſwered in the words of Appius Claudius, or to the ſame purpoſe: " Eludant nunc licet religiones. Quid " enim eſt, ſi pulli non paſcentur? Si ex cavea
                                    " tardius

" tardius exirent ? Si occinuerit avis? Parva ſunt
" hæc: ſed parva iſta non contemnendo majores
" noſtri maximam hanc rem fecerunt.".

CHAP. IV.

Of the Attributes of the Gods.

THE rule, which I mean to direct myſelf by,
in this argument, is to allow every thing to
be of human invention, which mankind can ſo
fully comprehend, that in certain circumſtances
they would neceſſarily act the ſame things over
again, without any other information than what
a proper exertion of their own faculties would
give. Thus, I think, they might have invented
language and writing, and ſeveral other things
which we have good reaſon to ſuppoſe were communicated ſupernaturally to the firſt man ; becauſe
I feel in myſelf a power of inventing ſuch things ;
and it ſeems hardly worth while to diſpute whether
I could have been put into a ſituation which would
have forced this power to act.

Nor are our notions of the wiſdom of God in
the leaſt debaſed by ſuch a conceſſion ; for the invention might have taken up more time, if mankind had been left to the exertion of their natural
abilities, than was conſiſtent with the circumſtances
of the world, or the plan which was then carrying
on ; eſpecially as, by their diſperſion afterwards,
they had full opportunity of exerting and diſ-
playing this part of their abilities.

In the ſame manner, though God revealed himſelf to the firſt man, every thing that was truly
ſupernatural was loſt amidſt the general corruption
which

which enfued; this introducing as great a confufion among the moral and religious principles of mankind, as was afterwards made in their language, fo that nothing but a few infignificant forms remained, analogous to what a common alphabet might be in languages eſſentially different.

It is true an antiquarian might trace a connection between two nations in ſome former period, from their making uſe of a common alphabet, though the languages were totally different. And it might be ſhewn from ſacrifices, and ſome other cuſtoms, that the heathen ſuperſtition ſprung originally from the firſt revelation. But as I reaſon only upon facts that are allowed on all ſides, without pretending to eſtabliſh directly ſuch as are controverted, by unbelievers, I ſhall allow the whole of the heathen ſuperſtition to be of human invention, becauſe they retained nothing but what ſuited their fancies; and I can ſee nothing in it above the power, or more properly, the weakneſs of man.

The heathens, therefore, would have the making of their own gods; and I am now to confider the materials that they would probably make uſe of for this purpoſe. The character of the gods would be formed according to the prejudices of mankind as to happineſs, and the uſe and occafions which they had for their interpofitions.

The gods could not anſwer the ends of their votaries, unleſs they were ſuppoſed able to do every thing which could be required of them; having at the ſame time every advantage which any man could wifh for.

They would aſcribe powers and faculties to their gods, not by reaſoning from effects to cauſes; or, in other words, they would not, by confidering what
they

they had done, infer what they might do, but from prejudice and paſſion; that is, from their own wants and wiſhes they would give their gods every power and every enjoyment which their own circumſtances required, or their moſt extravagant wiſhes could ſuggeſt. Becauſe, whoever attends to the notions of the vulgar among ourſelves (and there was a time when all mankind belonged to that claſs, in point of underſtanding) will find that the powers which they conceive to belong to the ſupernatural beings of their own formation, are ſuch as every one may have been fool enough to wiſh for in ſome part of his life: the power of conveying themſelves readily from place to place; of rendering themſelves inviſible and invulnerable; a great capacity of doing miſchief, and alſo of conferring benefits and favours. The witches of the vulgar among us, ride through the air, plunge to the bottom of the ſea, and perform other feats of the ſame kind.

Mankind would make their gods omnipotent in a certain ſenſe; at leaſt the chief of the gods would be ſo. For the world would never be content with one; though it may be ſaid that the idea of many, ſuppoſes firſt the idea of one: but mankind could never be ſuppoſed to reſt here, unleſs a man could be ſuppoſed to place his confidence for ſupport and protection in one rather than in a multitude, and prefer a ſolitary ſituation to the mirth and jollity of ſociety.

The chief of the gods therefore (for there would undoubtedly be a chief) would have abſolute power over gods and men, as far as was conſiſtent with the nature of ſuch *beings:* In ſhort, he could do what Homer allows to Jupiter, or rather what Jupiter takes to himſelf in the beginning of the
eighth

eighth book of the Iliad. And I confider Homer as much better authority for the natural and generally received attributes of the gods, than any philosopher whatever; for what this poet delivers was certainly the general opinion upon thefe fubjects; nor is it to be imagined, that an author who has reprefented his human characters with fuch propriety, would have done lefs juftice to his gods.

Inftead of being at the trouble of going fo very high as refined fpeculations, for difcovering the fource of the notions, which the heathens had of their gods, it even appears that we fhall not be much out of our way, in fuppofing that they copied them directly from the great and rich men of this world, with fuch an increafe of power as their nature and fituation gave them. And if thefe notions were once eftablifhed, legiflators would labour in vain to remove them, even when they felt their pernicious effects in a fociety. For as Cato fays in Livy, " Nihil enim in fpeciem fal-
" lacius eft quam prava religio; ubi Deorum nu-
" men prætenditur fceleribus, fubit animum ti-
" mor, ne fraudibus humanis vindicandis, divini
" juris aliquid immixtum violemus." Here it is to be obferved, that the wickednefs of the action could not be alledged as any proof that it was not committed by their gods; for the ftrefs is not laid upon the *fcelus*, but upon the *fraus humana*: if the gods did the wicked action there was no help, nor did they run any hazard of lofing their character; or rather from the expreffion *divini juris*, it feems as if the Romans confidered the committing of wicked actions as a part of the privileges of the gods. And fo far would this prejudice be carried, that I am perfuaded it would be in vain to look for morality as making any part of the character

of

of the heathen gods. Nor is it probable that Cicero, who was a very religious man, intends any reflection upon Jupiter, when he ſays of Clodius, with a ſneer, that he might call himſelf Jupiter, becauſe he had his ſiſter for his wife.

It would be impoſſible for men to live together in ſociety, unleſs they had the ſame general notions of morality ; and the rules derived from the moſt obvious and neceſſary of theſe, would make the very terms of their union, and which they muſt agree to preſerve inviolate, or ruin would be the conſequence ; though each individual might, upon occaſion, look upon the obſervance of ſuch rules as a great hardſhip ; and would, in all probability, endeavour to confine the obſervance of them to as narrow limits as poſſible : as for inſtance, firſt to his own ſociety, regarding himſelf as excuſed from the obſervance of them, when any member of another ſociety was concerned, eſpecially where it could be done with impunity. And notwithſtanding this privilege, he would find his morality ſtill too heavy for him, without ſome farther indulgences : and accordingly he would eaſily get the better of many ſcruples where his inferiors were concerned ; who would be obliged to yield from a ſenſe of inferiority and want of protection.

This liberty of relaxing his rules of morality, every man would certainly conſider as an advantage, and a total exemption of courſe, he would regard as the greateſt privilege ; " Qui nolunt " occidere quenquam poſſe volunt." It is not therefore to be imagined, that mankind would degrade their notions of the gods, by annexing to their character ſuch a troubleſome thing as morality.

Without

Without paffions, according to vulgar conception there could be no enjoyment; and this enjoyment would be confined to the gratification of
paffions, refembling the moft turbulent of their
own : and a *Being* who could not indulge his paffions, could never come up to the vulgar idea of
a god.

A heathen god, therefore, is exempted from
being a moral agent ftrictly fpeaking, though he
might be obliged to conform to fome rules among
his own fraternity, and be liable to have fome
demands of gratitude made upon him for the
affiduous attendance and refpect of mortals. And
the fyftem of Epicurus, which I think is abfurdly
confidered as a fyftem of Atheifm, is only the refinement and farther profecution of the fame principles, carried indeed fo far as to be inconfiftent
with the very ends of all religion. Laertius com-
mends Epicurus for many virtues, particularly for
his piety and devotion towards the gods : in which
I can eafily conceive he might be fincere, for I fee
juft as good a foundation for his piety, as for his
natural philofophy; both of which are only inftances of the extravagance and inconfiftency of
the human mind.

We may therefore hold it for a rule, that while
the power of the gods remained unqueftionable,
their morality would never be inquired into. And
borrowing all their notions from the fame fource,
men would very naturally afcribe to the gods all
the capricious foibles of the rich and powerful.
And to this purpofe, there is a remarkable paffage
in Valerius Maximus; it is the reflection which he
makes upon the religious exercifes of the Romans,
which they performed after the battle of Cannæ,

in

in the following words : " Qua quidem conſtantia
" obtinendæ religionis, magnus injeſtus eſt cœ-
" leſtibus *rubor* ulterius adverſus eam ſæviendi
" gentem ; quæ ne ihjuriarum quidem accrbitate
" ab eorum cultu abſterreri poterat." And when
we add concerning this boaſted devotion, that a
part of it, as we learn from Livy, conſiſted in
the ſacrifice of two men and two women, it will
not greatly raiſe our notions of the morality of the
heathen gods.

And this will enable us to account for a wonderful circumſtance in the heathen creed, namely,
that the moſt devout never ſuppoſed their own
moral actions could influence their deities. Politicians and moraliſts made many attempts to graft
ſomething of morality upon the common ſuperſtitions, but the ſtock was ſo unnatural, that it never
produced any fruit. Their prieſts told them that
they muſt ſacrifice ſuch a victim, which muſt be
killed in ſuch a place, in ſuch a manner, and with
ſuch a knife ; but not a word is to be found of
their promiſing them the favour of the gods, if
they repented of their ſins, and led better lives.

Now this being the character of the gods, and
as men chuſe to have as many friends as poſſible
among the great, ſo a number of divinities would
be the wiſh of the multitude ; and the number of
the gods would be alſo increaſed, according to the
notion which they had of their power and dignity ; ſome offices would be too mean and inconſiſtent with the rank of ſome gods, which is very
evident from the heathen *mythology*; and likewiſe
they would increaſe their number, not chuſing to
overload them with a multiplicity of affairs, which
might diſtract their attention, or interrupt them
in the courſe of their pleaſures or amuſements.

Abſurd

Abfurd as thefe notions may appear to be, and certainly are, whoever examines human nature attentively, will neverthelefs fee reafon to think them juft. We who have the advantage of the light diffufed through the world by the Chriftian Religion, form a very wrong eftimate of the human character upon fuch fubjects as thefe; and will not allow ourfelves to fee into half its weakneffes; for where fear and uncertainty both take place and affault the mind, it is aftonifhing what idiots mankind are, and what extravagant imaginations they will adopt for truth. Nothing but the Chriftian Religion can, or ought, to drive fuch phantoms from the minds of men. Human nature wants their aid, impotent as they are; nor can any degree of knowledge, which we are capable of acquiring naturally, fupply their place. And I am well perfuaded that many of the heathens, even the wifeft of them, were really in earneft, when it has been fuppofed that they were acting a part, and humouring the vulgar. The vulgar, which properly fpeaking, includes every body, and who have been the inftruments of making and unmaking all the idols in the world, according as they have been inftructed or mifled. So that a knowledge which was not in fome way or other fuited to their capacity, could bring about no great revolution or reformation in human affairs. The opinions of the philofophers were only a cloak to conceal their ignorance; and if they were able to fupport an opinion of greater knowledge, this was all that they defired: Real knowledge was never communicated by mankind in the form of myftery; when we have made a real difcovery, we are even anxious that all the world fhould know it.

- When

When the Chriſtian Religion had entirely deſ-troyed the heathen gods, the different ſects of philoſophers joined in the triumph, particularly the Epicureans, and ſeem to put on an appearance of independence, by new modelling their ſyſtems, with the aſſiſtance of this light.

The human mind is not capable of receiving ſuch contradictions, as that a thing ſhould be longer and ſhorter at the ſame time than another thing; but it is very capable of reconciling the reaſonings of Plato, or even of Epicurus, with the gods of the vulgar.

From the light which we have got at preſent, we may be able to ſhew, that many things are ab-ſurd and inconſiſtent, two of which ought not to be believed at the ſame time; yet it will by no means follow that they were not both univerſally believed. If you invent philoſophic principles, which in their conſequences ought to deſtroy cer-tain ſuperſtitions, the hopes and fears of mankind, and perhaps your own hopes and fears, will bid defiance to the conſequences.

Even while a man is labouring to overturn one ſpecies of ſuperſtition, he may not have leiſure to conſider, what other kinds he is expoſing himſelf to if he ſucceed. And if he were aſked, ſuppoſing his work compleated, what he meant to ſubſtitute in its ſtead? He might be very much puzzled with conſequences, whether he anſwered ſomething or nothing.

The truth is, the faculties and circumſtances of men require ſomething, and no one has a right or authority to ſubſtitute his viſions in preference to thoſe of others; or if they were ſubſtituted, they would be but new modes of ſuperſtition, it being above human power to apply the proper remedy to this infirmity.

C H A P.

CHAP. V.

Of the Religious Principles of the Jews.

THE account, which has been here given of the religious opinions of mankind, will be found to be agreeable to experience, as far as the nature of this argument requires, without any exception, speaking of bodies of men or nations, but the people of the Jews ; and probably upon a nearer inspection, even they will serve to confirm this reasoning, at the same time that they stand an exception to the conclusion drawn from it.

I have considered such opinions as flowing naturally from the joint operation of our faculties and circumstances in this world, and consequently incapable of reformation by any human power, though it is the very nature of such opinions to be unstable, and variable, and continually shifting from one absurdity to another. And the probabilities, possibilities, inconsistencies, contradictions, and imaginary principles of the different sects of philosophers, were least of all likely to fix the opinions of mankind. If the Jews had dealt in the same kind of principles, even if the whole nation had equalled the refinement of the most acute philosophers, I never should have thought it necessary to consider them as a distinct class of men from the rest of the world.

But we find among the Jews a positive assertion, that there is only one God, the Creator, the Maker, the Preserver of every thing : Eternal as to his duration ; Omnipotent as to his power ; and essentially present every where : lording it

over

over every thing according to his will and pleaſure, yet executing every thing according to infinite power, wiſdom, goodneſs and juſtice: No reſpecter of perſons, but, without caprice or partiality, rewarding every one according to his deeds. Not even the poſſibility, much leſs the ſlighteſt probability of the interference, or the exiſtence of any other god is allowed in the Jewiſh ſcheme of Religion.

But do theſe ſublime, and as I may call them, unnatural truths, appear to be the fruits of the ſpeculations and obſervations of this people? By no means, quite the contrary: for every circumſtance in their hiſtory confirms us in a different opinion. Nay, ſo far was this from being a natural ſentiment, that it required very extraordinary, or rather ſupernatural means, to impreſs them with it at firſt, and preſerve it among them afterwards, even when delivered as the moſt important of all truths.

And indeed, ſo remarkably ſingular did their opinions and behaviour appear to thoſe who contented themſelves with a ſuperficial view of the jewiſh policy, that they could hardly believe the Jews to be of the ſame ſpecies with the reſt of mankind. And this ſeems to have been the opinion of every nation who knew them, founded upon that unſociable diſpoſition, which made it impoſſible for them to incorporate with the reſt of mankind.

Antiquity was well acquainted with their opinions and character, as far as they choſe to inform themſelves, or rather as far as their prejudices would ſuffer them to receive information. And it was not for want of opportunity, but becauſe they had not abilities to comprehend it, that ſuch a pure ſyſtem of *Theiſm*, or what has been abſurdly called

natural

natural Religion, had no effect towards curing the antients of their fuperititions. Nay, the reft of mankind received the principles and pretenfions of the Jews not with a bare indifference, much lefs with the fpirit of philofophers, but with the moft abfurd and malignant interpretation, which the moft outrageous prejudice could invent.

Nor is this by any means to be wondered at, according to the view of the fubject which I have taken, but is rather to be expected, fince fuch opinions proceeded from nothing in human nature, and confequently muft have been unintelligible to thofe who trufted entirely to that for their guide. Such of the antients as might be difpofed to examine them, would confider opinions fo very different from their own, as the effect of fome capricious humour in this people; and inftead of regarding the pofitive and confiftent nature of this Religion, as the marks of a conviction derived from extraordinary evidence, they would fuppofe it the fruits of an obftinate temper, which led them to contradict the Reafon, Feelings, and Religion of the reft of mankind. And meafuring every thing by their own unfettled notions, the beft eftablifhed truths would appear the moft unreafonable.

The patrons of what is called natural Religion, ought to read with aftonifhment thofe parts of Tacitus in which he treats with the greateft indifference, or rather contempt, the religious opinions of the Jews. This man of a philofophic turn of mind, gives the following account of the Jewifh Religion; " Judæi (fays he) mente fola, " unumque numen intelligunt. Profanos qui " Deùm imagines, mortalibus materiis, in fpe- " ciem hominis effingunt. Summum illud et " æternum,

" æternum, neque mutabile neque interiturum.
" Igitur nulla fimulacra urbibus fuis, nedum
" templis funt." And the reafon which he gives
for their adopting thefe fimple and elevated notions fo worthy of the Deity, and fo agreeable to
right reafon, fhew the powerful effects of prejudice over the minds of men of the greateft abilities; and that all men, when carried beyond the
little circle of their knowledge, are as it were
carried back to their infant ftate, with this
only difference, that they have loft their teachable
difpofition.

The heathen deities, according to Tacitus, are
not forfaken by the Jews, upon any rational conviction of the falfity and abfurdity of idolatry and
fuperftition : for it feems they had no better reafon
to induce them to change their religious opinions,
and 'take up thofe juft now mentioned (which this
author feems to look upon, as a kind of Atheifm)
than this, that Mofes advifes them to forfake both
gods and men, becaufe they themfelves were abandoned by both. For he adds, " Plurimi auctores
" confentiunt, ut orta per Ægyptum tabe quæ
" corpora fœdaret, regem Ocharin, adito Ham-
" monis oraculo, remidium petentem, purgare
" regnum; et id genus hominum, ut invifum
" diis, alias in terras avehere juffum. Sic conquæ-
" fitum collectumque vulgus, poftquam vaftis
" locis relictum fit, ceteris per lacrymas torpen-
" tibus, Mofen, unum exulum, monuiffe ne
" quam deorum hominumve opem expectarent,
" ab utrifque deferti, fed fibimet ut duci cœlefti
" crederent, primo cujus auxilio credentes, pre-
" fentes miferias pepuliffent."

According to this account it might be expected,
that Mofes would either abolifh all religious cere-

monies,

monies, and eftablifh a nation of Atheifts, or elfe take fuch meafures as would put all things in readinefs for his own *Apotheofis*. However, this it feems was not the cafe; for he adds, " Mofes " quo fibi in pofterum gentem firmaret, novos " ritus, contrariofque cæteris mortalibus indidit. " Profana illic omnia quæ apud nos facra. Rurfum " conceffa apud illos quæ nobis incefta."

Here we fee, in as clear a manner as words can exprefs it, that this author, though one of the acuteft of antiquity, has no conception of the truth, fimplicity, and fublimity of the Jewifh Religion; but imagines that it was the invention of a man, not even himfelf convinced of its truth, nor fenfible of its purity and fublimity: who adopted it not from reafon, or plaufibility, or any intrinfic merit or fitnefs in the opinions themfelves to anfwer any ends which he might have in view; but he adopted them from a fpirit of contradiction, in a fplenetic humour, merely out of oppofition to other nations, who held the Jews in deteftation for thefe very principles. Which makes it highly improbable that the heathens could have fhaken off their idolatry and fuperftition, by the affiftance of any natural means, even by the greateft degree of cultivation of which the human faculties are capable without fupernatural affiftance: for the man who firft did it would have been regarded as a perfon of a defpicable and abandoned character: As the fame author fays, fpeaking of the fame people, and the fame religious principles, that it was only the moft profligate and unprincipled who adopted fuch opinions. " Nam peffi- " mus quifque, fpretis religionibus patriis, tribu- " ta et ftipes illuc congerebant." And again, " Tranfgreffi in morem eorum, idem ufurpant,

" nec

" nec quidquam prius imbuuntur quam contem-
" nere deos, &c." So that we find this contempt of the gods conſtantly inſiſted on, as the
circumſtance upon which the chief ſtreſs is laid :
and it appears of itſelf of ſuch weight, as to determine this author to conclude that thoſe, who
became converts to ſuch opinions, were loſt to
every thing that is good.

Tacitus, perhaps, might have been able to accommodate his reaſon to the principles of Epicurus, and think that he was paying a compliment
to the gods, by taking the government of the
world out of their hands; but his prejudices
could not bear that contempt of them, which is
the very firſt ſtep to a proper knowledge of the
true God. But here ſome pert infidel will be apt
to interrupt me, by aſking, can I believe that a po-
litician ſo very acute could be liable to ſo much
weakneſs ? Why not : when this very ſame poli-
tician has given us a proof of the moſt contemptible weakneſs, beſides ſhewing himſelf to be a ſlave
to the loweſt vulgar prejudice, in his pretence to
aſſign a cauſe for the length of our days in ſum-
mer. And the ſame excuſe for his abſurdity would
ſerve upon both ſubjects ; namely, that he was
ignorant of the true principles of Religion and
Aſtronomy.

Thoſe who had nothing but the common ſuperficial obſervation to direct them, and who
looked at the Jews through ſuch a thick miſt of
prejudice, had no other concluſion to draw, but
that they were a different ſpecies from the reſt of
the human race. And yet if we turn to their
hiſtory, as we have it authentic in the Bible, they
will appear to be the ſame kind of men with the
reſt of the world, yet deſerving the moſt ſerious
attention of all mankind.

In

In this hiſtory, it is eaſy to be ſeen that they are exactly of the ſame diſpoſition with the reſt of the world, and at leaſt as prone to idolatry as their neighbours; becauſe it requires ſupernatural efforts frequently repeated to bring them to a ſenſe of their ſituation, which they never rightly underſtood, and to preſerve thoſe important truths communicated to them, and which they were to be the means of preſerving, and communicating to the world at a time appointed. Nay, thoſe who will read with care, the awful threatnings, and actual interpoſitions of heaven, muſt be ſurpriſed to find that they had no greater effect; as they were, by no means, ſufficient for keeping this nation from falling into all the idolatrous and ſuperſtitious practices of their neighbours.

Nor was it the mere vulgar only who had occaſion to be thus reſtrained; but the very wiſeſt of all their kings falls into the ſame ſnare; which, beſides proving many other things, clears this plan of all ſuſpicion of human contrivance; as one of its greateſt viſible ſupporters as a king and an inſpired writer, deſerts his charge, and falls in with the abominations of the nations.

The great and conſtant care taken to keep the Jews from mixing with ſtrangers, and that even this was often ineffectual, proves how natural the groſſeſt kinds of ſuperſtition are to the human mind. When it is ſeen that the immediate preſence of the Deity in ſigns and wonders, and exemplary puniſhments, could not keep this people to right principles, and preſerve them from the infection of idolatry. And ſurely this is ſufficient to prove that proper notions of God and his attributes, are beyond the power of man to attain to, by any effort of his own; or even if they were delivered

I　　　　　　　　　　　　　　to

to him as the truths of natural Religion, that his circumſtances and his paſſions, would be leading him daily to pervert and corrupt them.

ᐧ In affairs which come properly within our power, mankind make a very reſpectable figure: there is a progreſs and variety in the world as to government, arts, and ſciences; even human actions and events are connected together, and follow conſequentially, leading from ſmall and inſenſible beginnings, to ſuch concluſions and improvements, as could never have been expected or imagined. Here the human race ſhew that they have been in action, and that what has been done, muſt have been the work of time and opportunity; the employment of many hands, and the invention of many heads. But when we turn to the ſubject of Religion, we even diſcover a barrenneſs of invention, and a poverty of imagination, and inſtead of variety and connexion, a number of dull, ſenſeleſs, detached conceits, which might have been the conception of a moment, and the ſimultaneous production of a diſtempered imagination. Human nature ſeems ſo completely exhauſted by the birth of ſuch a *monſter*, that ſhe has no farther power to provide for this offspring of hers, than by beſtowing upon it ſome of the worſt of her own paſſions.

THE END OF THE FIRST BOOK.

B O O K

B O O K II.

*Containing a Philosophical Estimate of the
Situation and Circumstances of Men, as to
temporal Advantages, by considering them
as under the Protection, though Subject to
the arbitrary Disposal of God.*

C H A P. I.

The Idea of this Book.

A Philosophical inquiry may be carried on upon
different principles, and with a view to
answer different ends.

The question may be, Is the effect an adequate
measure for the cause assigned, so that in subjects
of computation the one may be substituted for the
other ? And whenever this can be shewn to be the
case, I conceive the discovery to be within the
reach of the human faculties. But it is to be observed, before this can be done with propriety, that
the cause must be such as can produce that effect
only, and neither one greater or less ; that is, the
cause must exhaust itself in the effect, and cannot
avoid exhausting itself, otherwise it would be impossible to draw any certain conclusions. To prove
supernatural things to be cause and effect in this
manner, would be to destroy all distinction between
natural and supernatural events : as the effects produced

duced would not be the voluntary act of any agent, but would follow neceſſarily from ſome determinate ſyſtem of things: and then, the diſcovery of any ſuch operations ought not to be conſidered as a revelation, ſeeing it would depend upon the accidental or intentional placing the cauſe in the ſituation proper for producing its effects.

A certain quantity of water will move a certain machine; the reſiſtance of the machine is a proper meaſure for the force of the water: a certain ſpace of ground produces a certain quantity of grain; the quantity of grain is a meaſure for the fruitful force of the ground, and ſo in other inſtances. Such diſcoveries increaſe the powers of man, and give him a kind of command over nature, by putting him in a certain degree into a ſtate of independence. And this makes us wiſh to reduce every thing to this kind of knowledge, being in hopes of acquiring, as it were, a little dominion of our own, where we might have nothing to fear but mechanical cauſes and their neceſſary conſequences.

A little experimenting philoſopher, by drawing a few ſparks from an *electrical machine*, takes up the conceit that he has diſarmed heaven of its thunder, and thinks the moſt prudent thing the world can do is to renounce the protection of God, and put themſelves under his. If we were careful to make a proper eſtimate of our knowledge, we would ſtifle in their birth, a number of ſuch little, impious conceits, which are produced by the force of novelty inſtead of demonſtration. For as far as my experience reaches, I find knowledge deſpiſed in proportion to its certainty. Whether it be that the human imagination muſt have ſomething to work upon, and would be entirely out of its element in a ſtate of

certainty,

certainty, or whether it arifes from a reftlefsnefs of mind, which will not fuffer us to be contented in any condition. However this may be, it is my opinion, that, if we were rendered independent of all the *material* agents in the univerfe, there is fuel enough in the human paffions to fet the world in a flame, and difturb the peace of individuals and whole focieties.

But the very ferious part which every one feels he has affigned him, joined to the fmall progrefs which has been made in tracing effects to their real caufes, obliges us to give up fuch conceits of independence, and view the univerfe in a very different light from a machine, which may be taken to pieces, and put together again by human power, or even by human imagination. And this fenfe of our weaknefs, gives rife to another kind of philofophical inquiry, which directly adds nothing to our command over nature, but rather fhews us how dependent we are: and is particularly ufeful for giving us a command over ourfelves, and efpecially neceffary for our circumftances and fituation in the world.

This inquiry does not confift in an attempt to difcover the caufes of things, fo as to meafure the caufes and effects by each other; but rather, taking the facts as we find them, without inquiring into the mode of making things, to content ourfelves with forming a character of the caufe or caufes that produced them: and this is all that can be done when the caufe is a free agent: becaufe a defigning intelligent caufe can never be inveftigated to perfection by its effects. To pretend that it can produce nothing but what it has produced, and muft produce at ftated times; or fuch things as follow by way of natural confequence, deftroys every idea of defign or intelligence, unlefs we
should

ſhould ſuppoſe the cauſe ſo impotent as to have
its effects counteracted by the nature of things, or
the power of man ; and thus confined to certain
limits, and a certain manner of acting. But inſtead
of pretending to comprehend the *Supreme Being* in
this manner, a man will often find occaſion to
repent of his raſhneſs, in being too confident that
he could thus comprehend his fellow-creatures.

We may examine whether, to the beſt of our
apprehenſion, there is that conſiſtency among the
things of this world, that they can ſtand together
as parts of the ſame plan ; and alſo whether they
have ſuch a harmony with the feelings and faculties of mankind, as to create in us a great degree
of pleaſure : for if this be true, it ought to lead us
to conclude, that we were not overlooked in the
contrivance of this mighty fabric of the univerſe.
However, we ought conſtantly to keep in mind,
what almoſt every thing tends to teach us, that
our buſineſs in this world is not to look for palaces,
but to ſeek for ſhelter from the ſtorm which the
turbulence of our paſſions, and the weakneſs of
our underſtanding have raiſed.

To be obliged to live in a world with every thing
contradicting our ſenſes and feelings, if it failed to
produce idiotiſm, would be a ſtate of abſolute torment ; though to other *beings* of a different ſpecies,
every thing might appear to be diſpoſed according
to the greateſt wiſdom and regularity. Our opinions, therefore, upon ſuch a ſubject as the attributes of God when in ſuch circumſtances, though
they would be melancholy truths to us, yet would
they be relative to our views and ſenſations, rather
than to the real nature of things, and might lead
us to fix a general character upon the Author of
nature which he did not deſerve.

Nay,

Nay, if we were only ignorant of our *original* and *deſtination*, many things might be diſagreeable to us as ſenſible creatures, which would appear to be wiſe and good, when the ends which they were to anſwer came to be known and underſtood. And all this might depend upon our being *arbitrarily* placed in certain circumſtances, which could neither be foreſeen nor inferred from any thing, having no other cauſe but the bare ſovereign will and pleaſure of the Author of nature.

And this conſideration takes the ſubject entirely out of our hands, and reduces us to the character and office of *ſpectators*, who can only take ſuch a view of the univerſe as it has pleaſed God to preſent to us, and indulge us with faculties to comprehend. And the great probability that this is true, ought to convince us that any ſyſtem which we can build, would reſt upon too ſandy a foundation to give us the leaſt encouragement to be confident or dogmatical. A ſenſible creature fixing abſolute truth, is the man with his candle examining the ſun-dial to diſcover the hour of the night.

In the laſt book I have obſerved how unfit we are naturally, from our paſſions and circumſtances, even to form a character of the cauſes which produce the different effects in this world, particularly ſuch as more immediately concern ourſelves. The gods into whoſe hands the heathens delivered up the government of the univerſe, are imaginary and impotent, and their characters immoral, contradictory and abſurd; and yet in certain circumſtances, ſuch is the weakneſs of human nature, the wiſeſt men put themſelves under their protection.

Mankind are diſpoſed in ſpeculation to extend their reaſon very far, but in practice they always contract

contract it to its natural and narrow limits; and upon the moſt important and preſſing occaſions abandon it entirely. We may be truſted with the choice of our food, or to ſettle the proportions and dimenſions of our habitations; but we require a ſupernatural direction and information, when our own character, and that of the Supreme Being, is the ſubject of our conſideration. And as God has condeſcended to reveal to us both his own character and ours, in as far as we are concerned, it will be much to our comfort and advantage, to take a view of ourſelves and the univerſe, aſſiſted by this new light. But as a gradual emerſion from our natural darkneſs, ſeems to agree better with our faculties, and will ſhock our prejudices leſs than a ſudden ſally into broad day-light, I propoſe in this book to conſider the general revealed character of God, and the real poſitive, preſent and temporal advantages which we enjoy by being under the protection, though ſubject to the government, and left to the arbitrary diſpoſal of God. And although the fact and truth will remain the ſame, whatever may be the reſult of our ſpeculations, yet if we ſee reaſon to be content with our ſituation, and diſcover rational grounds for future hopes, the change will be very conſiderable in ourſelves, as ſuch meditations will prepare the mind for receiving the evidence of the Chriſtian Religion with leſs prejudice; and are beſides of wonderful ſervice for enabling a man to regulate his own imaginations, which, if not reſtrained within proper bounds, are capable, in certain circumſtances, of doing infinite miſchief to himſelf and the world, whether he acts the Atheiſt or the Enthuſiaſt.

E   CHAP,

CHAP. II.

Containing some general Observations upon the Manner in which it has pleased God to reveal himself to the World.

WE find in the history of the Jews, that they were taught to believe in one God only, who is represented as the Creator and Preserver of the whole Universe, infinitely powerful, wise, good and just, acting through all ages and every where without restraint or controul. But we find at the same time, that these principles were not discovered or communicated to the Jewish nation, in the same manner as we are taught or discover such things as human reason and ingenuity, aided by the common appearances and accidents of the world, may discover, invent, and communicate.

It is delivered as a fact by Moses, that God had revealed himself to him, in a manner, which conveyed an information to his mind, of the same kind as that which one man receives from another by words, to distinguish it from that kind of knowledge which we acquire consequentially. It is true the rest of the Jews were kept at a greater distance; and yet they were not left to general consequential reasoning; and therefore Moses does not prepare them to expect arguments only in the way of scientific inference, as proofs of his assertions; but to look for a full and sensible confirmation of them in the signs and wonders which were to be exhibited; which would be suited to, and demonstrative, of the character which God had assumed to himself. And the whole Jewish po-

5   licy

lity may be regarded as contrived by God, on purpose to give a proper difplay of his character to mankind. And in the courfe of the hiftory of the Ifraelites, we have his unity, power, wifdom, goodnefs and juftice afferted and proved by facts; but chiefly that he has a will, or is a free agent in the moft extenfive fenfe of the word, acting by no neceffity either of nature or principle, but according to his own fovereign will and pleafure.

When the Jews neglected or difregarded thofe important truths, their attention was not called to the common arguments of reafon to convince them of their miftake, or as grounds for cenfuring and punifhing them for their neglect; but their paffions were applied to and alarmed by figns and wonders addreffed immediately to their fenfes. The power of God was not left to reach their minds as it might appear in argumentative confequences, from the general plan of the world, but was majeftically exhibited to their fenfes, and by them conveyed directly to their minds by an occafional exertion of his almighty power. And thefe were fo frequent, and fo well eftablifhed among this people, as to form a regular habit of thinking, in the fame manner as our education leads us to wifh for a certain habitual form of argument upon which we have been taught to ground our conviction. The Jews fought after a fign, juft as naturally as the Greeks expected fyftematical reafoning.

And notwithftanding what has been faid to the contrary, fuch an evidence as this which the Jews received feems abfolutely neceffary; for the prefent world which is at enmity with God could furnifh nothing adequate to this purpofe. For properly fpeaking, it was fuch arguments as tend to prove that there are gods which mifled mankind, for they

never

never feem to have been blind to the common arguments of natural Religion. It was the exiftence
of one God only, with a particular character, of
which they needed to be informed and convinced :
and this conviction human reafon, fettered as we
find it by human paffions, and blinded by prejudices, never could attain to, nor indeed even bear
it after it was difcovered, as appears remarkably in
the cafe of the Jews, who have it forced upon them
by irrefiftible evidence contrary to their inclinations.   God's dealings with them is not to bring
them to a conviction or belief, that there are fome
god or gods, but to cure them, and the whole
world by their example, of that natural propenfity
which all mankind have to idolatry.   " I am the
Lord, and there is none elfe," is the doctrine conftantly infifted on : and that this doctrine is true,
is proved to them by figns and wonders : that as
they were convinced by the appearances of nature,
and their own fenfations and reflections, that there
muft be gods, or active and intelligent natures,
producing, directing, and influencing the things of
this world, whom for want of information they endued with paffions fitted to the groffnefs of their
own conceptions and wifhes, fo the only poffible
means by which this prejudice could be removed,
would be by exhibiting a ftronger evidence in proof
that there was but one God of fuch a particular
character.

And it is this character which mankind diflike,
as they can have no profpect of indulging their
paffions, or gratifying their particular evil humours while the government of the univerfe is in
fuch hands.   The heathens heard with pleafure
every ftory in which their gods were reprefented
as capricious, and without morality.   We have a
dread

dread of perfection from a conſciouſneſs of our own infirmity: and provided he had ſufficient power to protect us, we would place ourſelves under the government of a man ſubject to paſſions like our own, inſtead of chuſing a perfect character, who would curb our paſſions, and be a critique upon our conduct.

The Supreme Being may be conſidered in the plan of Religion, as creating a new world, and exhibiting it for the inſpection, information, and conviction of mankind, upon a ſubject to which they are naturally ſo averſe, and in which they alone of all this lower creation are any way intereſted. A world in which this nation of the Jews were at firſt to be the principal actors, ſtrongly ſupported and carried through all dangers and difficulties; and theſe not ſuch as fall in the way of the generality of mankind; but which this people were evidently led into for a particular purpoſe. And yet every thing yields before them, without almoſt any effort of their own, or rather to efforts which, according to the regular courſe of human affairs, were totally inadequate to the purpoſes intended and the effects produced.

But this world of Religion is not made after the model of the natural world, which came completely into being at once *by the word of his power*; and as ſoon as God had ſaid *let there be light*, all its parts were fit for the inſpection of men. Religion has a gradual progreſs, proceeding from ſmall and obſcure beginnings, and growing up to perfection by degrees, which ſhews that God can perform his work ſlowly and in time, as well as inſtantaneouſly; and this work is not yet prepared for human comprehenſion, being a plan that the angels deſire to exerciſe their ſpeculations upon.

E 3 The

The reafonings from final caufes and the fitnefs of things, as exhibited in the material world, will give us no information upon this fubject, even if the plans were entirely fimilar ; unlefs one could fay, that a man by reading the hiftory of the Jews, was qualified to write the hiftory of England without any other materials. It is true the general attributes of power, wifdom and goodnefs, are deeply marked in what exifts, and is exhibited to us every day ; but, unlefs we could be fatisfied with the prefent moment, we are left to guefs and conjecture about our future condition. And the wifeft of the heathens furnifh us full proof how diftant thefe guefses and conjectures would be from the real matter of fact.

The arguments for a providence and the final caufes of things, is as full in Cicero's book *De natura Deorum*, as can be defired ; and it does not appear to me, fetting afide what has been borrowed from revelation, that any thing really new has been added to the argument fince : and therefore fome people have imagined, from the conviction that they themfelves have found from this reafoning, that many important queftions might be determined and finally fettled among mankind, independent of revelation.

But they ought to have drawn a quite contrary conclufion : for as thefe arguments in fact did not fettle the opinions of the antients upon fuch fubjects, they fhould have rather inferred that fuch arguments of themfelves are incapable of fixing the opinions of men.

We deceive ourfelves upon fuch queftions: the mind is wonderfully prepared by revelation to liften with attention, and I may even fay with prejudice to this argument, and a conviction, which

if

if accurately traced to its ſource, will be found to ſpring from revelation, we are very well diſpoſed to conſider as produced by an effort of our own underſtanding, and this is a weakneſs which the infidels themſelves are particularly ſubject to.

It is the antients alone who could feel the force of ſuch arguments, uninfluenced by any other principles : and Cicero owns that they never produced a ſolid and determinate conviction, either in himſelf or any of his cotemporaries, upon the moſt important and neceſſary points : for their minds were bewildered amidſt probabilities and abſurdities ; which left them to chuſe not what was true, but what was moſt probable or leaſt abſurd. And as they had no facts to build upon, they were forced to ſhare the deſigns and contrivances of the affairs of this world, and the preſervation and regulation of things among a number of *divinities*.

The Chriſtian Religion, if it has not every where made mankind believers, yet it has extinguiſhed idolatry and ſuperſtition, in the antient ſenſe of theſe words, wherever it has been received. And this makes a material difference between us and the heathens, even when we are examining the ſame queſtion, by the ſame light, and upon the ſame principles, becauſe many prejudices are removed out of our way, which they found it impoſſible to conquer. And therefore revelation, whether true or falſe, has been of great ſervice to the world, and even to the infidels themſelves, for which they ought to make proper acknowledgements, by leaving them only a ſingle prejudice to combat, inſtead of ſuch a multitude as preſented themſelves to an infidel in the ages of idolatry ; inſtead of the labours of Hercules, they have got things reduced to the wiſh of Caligula.

E 4 CHAP.

CHAP. III.

Of the Power of God.

THE firſt thing which we find aſcribed to God, is a creative power. He made every thing out of nothing, not in the way of natural generation, nor as a cauſe produces its effects, ſo that in the ſame circumſtances the ſame effects muſt neceſſarily be produced; or in other words, not by the miniſtry of ſecond cauſes; but he made every thing, as it is expreſſed, by the word of his power. This expreſſion, though it does not teach us how to make a world, yet appears to me highly proper for correcting thoſe errors which we naturally fall into upon this ſubject. For it conveys to us very diſtinctly the idea, that the making of the univerſe was an arbitrary act, and not performed from neceſſity, nor according to any eternal relations, ſo as to be a work of contrivance in fitting and adjuſting means to ends; but that the things and their relations came into exiſtence together: or more accurately, perhaps, that the relations were poſterior to the things. It ſeems to me impious to ſuppoſe that there were laws of gravitation, and that God placed and adjuſted the material worlds according to thoſe laws. I know the general prejudices and habits of mankind are againſt this opinion; becauſe this is a power of which we can have no experimental proof, and for this reaſon the thing itſelf is beyond human conception, and conſequently the notion itſelf is not likely to be of human invention.

But

But this power of creation, though it can make and deſtroy ourſelves and every thing elſe, is not what is apt to fill the mind with the greateſt dread and terror; becauſe we are not ſufficiently acquainted with it, or its operations, to derive matter of fear from them. Yet in the operations of natural things, we meet with ſuch conſtant exertions of deſtructive power, as might be ſufficient to drive to diſtraction ſuch a *being* as man, ſo ſenſible of his ſituation, and ſo liable to accidents. And therefore we may naturally imagine that this attribute of God, would be the firſt to make a deep impreſſion upon mankind. We may make our firſt notions upon this ſubject, more rational and conſiſtent with the other parts of the character of the Supreme Being, but we can ſcarcely enlarge them ſo as to make this attribute of power an object of greater terror. Man is a timorous animal, and in his fright will give up or acknowledge any thing. The truth is, that even to the moſt rational courage, and the beſt informed underſtanding, the notion of irreſiſtible power muſt be terrible, and without ſome alleviation, would be inconſiſtent with every idea of happineſs.

C H A P. IV.

Of the Wiſdom of God.

WE ſhall now conſider the moſt natural and obvious method which the mind can probably take to eaſe itſelf of thoſe dreadful apprehenſions in the moſt effectual manner, which the diſcovery of an infinite power, acting only with ſuch materials as are to be found in the univerſe (to ſay
nothing

nothing of the unlimited power of creating others)
would neceffarily occafion to a creature fo fenfible
of its fituation as man is known to be : a creature
who not only feels in the moment of danger, but
who has the impreffion of the paft, and the dread
of the future, ftrongly imprinted on his mind :
whofe hopes and fears keep his mind in fuch a
conftant agitation, as can only be rendered tolerable, either by finking into a ftupid infenfibility,
or by rational meditation upon his fituation and
circumftances.

Now it feems natural to imagine, that thofe
men whofe faculties were fufficiently acute to perceive the full effort of that power which is difcoverable in the vifible operations of the univerfe,
would exert their ingenuity, and apply their obfervation, to find out in what manner this -power
produced its effects; whether at random, or according to any regular method, from which fomething like fixed rules might be formed.

If they found any reafon to fufpect that there
was no harmony among the things of the material
world, we may eafily conceive the ftate of their
minds, by recollecting our own condition and
feelings when in fituations where we are liable to
accidents from things that we apprehend to be
acting at random. For if the terror which a fingle
inftance produces be fo unfupportable; how dreadful muft it be if we were fo fituated with regard
to every thing.

And yet, could it only once be perceived, that
this power acts according to fixed rules, whatever
thofe rules might be; and although in many fituations we were more certain of our deftruction
than if we knew no fuch rules; if we could only
be pretty confident of our fafety in fome others,

the

the very conſideration, that things are governed by fixed laws, will afford a ſatisfaction to the mind which cannot be had from more favourable, but more uncertain circumſtances. And this makes many people wiſh to be expoſed to the blows of blind fate, who, they think, can only ſtrike according to the laws of matter and motion, than to put themſelves, with reſignation, under the di-rection of a powerful, intelligent being, who may reaſonably puniſh them for their offences.

Farther, if it ſhould appear that things are not only fixed to a certain degree, but that the laws by which the appearances of the univerſe are re-gulated, are in a kind of active ſtate, extending their tendency beyond the immediate effects pro-duced; that is, that ſuch a thing is done for the ſake of ſomething to be done afterwards, or in conſequence of ſomething that has been done be-fore, ſo as to furniſh us with the notion of con-trivance, this immediately leads us to an intelli-gent cauſe or cauſes: and a farther examination into the manner according to which theſe means are made to bring about their ends, will ſuggeſt different degrees of wiſdom, according as the means ſeem to be more or leſs fitted for anſwering their particular ends.

Now, if this wiſdom ſhould appear to be infi-nite, we have then got a rational and proper ba-lance for an infinite power; and muſt conclude that the whole of this power will be put into action, and made to produce the beſt effects poſſi-ble; and that we have nothing to fear from blind fate, or the ungovernable nature of things, becauſe theſe can do nothing againſt infinite power directed by infinite wiſdom.

It

It is true, it is impossible for us to reach to a knowledge of infinite wisdom, though we have sufficient instances before our eyes of astonishing degrees of power and wisdom, displayed in the general structure of the world, the regular motions of the heavenly bodies; and the means made use of to preserve the brittle and complicated parts of animal bodies, together with their formation, furnish astonishing instances of wisdom to the attentive and rational observer: and the connection and dependence which the things have upon each other, exhibit demonstrative marks of a plan. This view of the universe would certainly lead our minds up to God, were we not so strongly connected with this world from our earliest infancy.

For, first, we are connected with the inanimate parts of the creation by our bodies, which, in many respects, are subject to the same laws that the grossest parts of matter obey; a human body, and a log of wood, fall from the top of a precipice exactly in the same manner; and many such laws as this we are very well acquainted with, before we are capable of any very deep reflection. Self-preservation, the idea of which is so strongly implanted in our nature, will not suffer us to delay the acquiring a knowledge of the most obvious and necessary properties of matter, until we can be certain that this knowledge is derived from proper principles. And, secondly, we are connected with the material world by our passions, the most turbulent and craving of which have their gratification in the enjoyment of earthly things; and the ravenous nature of some passions prevents any nice discernment in the choice of such gratifications.

On

On the other hand, we are connected with heaven immediately only by our reaſon, and but remotely by our paſſions; and after habits acquired by an uniform experience have given us a conviction, or rather a confidence (for there is no argument in the caſe) of the ſtability of the laws of nature, even before the uſe of reaſon; and when the experimental gratification of the paſſions by ſenſible things, have led us to conſider ſpiritual gratifications as unſubſtantial, or perhaps viſionary, reaſon has too hard a taſk, when ſet to combat ſuch habits and prejudices. A man who has ſuch ſtrong conviction of the ſtability and certainty of the things of this preſent world, cannot readily fall in with the thoughts of a new heaven and a new earth. And nothing but a clear and poſitive revelation can conquer ſuch natural prejudices, by exhibiting greater rewards and puniſhments as a conſequence of our behaviour in what concerns the other world. And as remote and diſtant proſpects affect us but little, how admirably are theſe promiſes and threatenings brought forward by the uncertainty of death; for to the man of underſtanding they are always preſent, as every moment may be his laſt.

If any one ſhould think that it might have been better not to have the material world governed by ſuch fixed laws, and that a ſucceſſion of new things would have exhibited more wiſdom and power than to bring back the ſame things in a conſtant rotation. Probably there are beings to whoſe faculties ſuch a ſcene might be ſuited, but we enjoy great advantages by having the inanimate parts of the creation ſubject to very fixed laws. For even the dead and inactive parts of matter, from the very circumſtance of their being
dead

dead and inactive, difcover wonderful contrivance, when it is confidered how by this means they are fitted for the convenience of animals, and efpecially of man.

It requires time and attention to get acquainted with the nature and difpofition of animals; nor, when once difcovered, is it always the fame; for they are fometimes mifchievous, and fometimes harmlefs: or if the nature of all animals was as difficult to know as that of man, this world would be uninhabitable or intolerable.

What a condition fhould we be in, if we were doubtful, after a thoufand experiments, whether we might thruft our hand into the fire or the water with moft fafety, upon a well-grounded apprehenfion, that they might have changed their nature fince our laft experience of their qualities.

But all our knowledge that is properly our own acquifition, is founded in habits which it is impoffible to form, but by prefenting the fame things again and again to our obfervation. And when we confider what a wonderful harmony, what a beautiful and magnificent fcene this univerfe prefents to us, and how nicely all its parts are balanced by the fingle law of gravitation, a defign fufficiently extenfive prefents itfelf to our view, though the fame appearances are repeatedly exhibited to us, yet not oftener than is neceffary for the inftruction of fuch a frail and tranfitory creature as man. And the farther confideration, that the law of this gravitation regulates the motion of the planets, and alfo of the comets, which make fo large a circuit, and pafs over a kind of immenfity of fpace, furnifhes a beautiful argument to our purpofe; the operations being carried on upon a fcale fufficiently large to enable us, upon feeing the

the motions of the bodies that come within our obſervation, ſo nicely adjuſted, and the harmony, order, and dependence of the parts of ſo large a ſyſtem preſerved, to aſſent with reaſon as well as faith to thoſe ſublime expreſſions of *Scripture*, in which thoſe attributes of power and wiſdom are revealed ; ſuch appearances being a *ſenſible*, intelligible, beautiful, and pertinent commentary upon Revelation.

And thus the power of God, though infinite, acting upon matter according to fixed laws, and ſuch as diſcover infinite wiſdom and contrivance, loſes, by that circumſtance alone, much of the terror which it would otherwiſe occaſion to ſuch a creature as man.

CHAP. V.

Of the Goodneſs of God.

THE ſentiments, which naturally ariſe in our minds, upon conſidering the power of the Supreme Being as infinite, even when moderated, and all the terrors of them as it were ſubdued by the reflection, that this power is directed by wiſdom equally uncontrouled and unlimited, would nevertheleſs be mixed with much of dread, before a conviction that we ourſelves are ſo particularly the objects of God's regard, that we may believe upon good grounds, that both his power and his wiſdom will be finally directed to procure us the moſt ſolid and laſting advantages.

But if we are not only in the hands of a powerful, but likewiſe of a wiſe and good *Being*, who enjoys theſe perfections, not as confined by the

circum-

circumſtances of time, place, or opportunity, but in an unlimited degree, we may reſt well aſſured, that he will make every thing, even the moſt unfavourable circumſtances, turn to the advantage of his ſenſible and rational creatures.

The power and wiſdom of God could have been ſufficiently diſplayed in this world, by the contrivance and arrangement and creation of mere inanimate matter; but it would have been impoſſible, from the moſt exquiſite contrivance of this kind, to have ever arrived at any notion of goodneſs. Yet when we find ſo much of the creation conſiſting of ſenſible creatures, capable of pleaſure and pain, happineſs and miſery; by obſerving the proviſion that is made for gratifying the deſires of ſuch creatures, and by conſidering the nature and nnmber of thoſe deſires, we may, in ſome meaſure, pronounce the principle or *Being* to which they owe their exiſtence to be either perfect or imperfect; and the motives of the Maker of ſuch a world to be either good or evil; though ſuch concluſions ought always to be drawn, with a ſtrong impreſſion upon our minds of our own ſhortſightedneſs, and how little we are qualified to judge of infinite perfections.

However, we cannot err according to my plan, which recommends ſuch ſpeculations only as a commentary upon the Scriptures, and propoſes a view of natural appearances, and our own ſituation in this world, as the moſt effectual, and even the only method for bringing down to our capacities any conception of that character of himſelf which God has been pleaſed to reveal. And this ought to be conſidered as an inſtance of his goodneſs, that he does not oblige us to live entirely by faith; or if that could not well be conſiſtent with our

nature

nature and faculties, yet it is wonderful condefcenfion to have fet his character before us in fuch
a clear light, making it the immediate object of
our fenfes in fuch numberlefs inftances, when he
might have put us upon the neceffity of taking his
own word for it. And nothing can be a greater
proof of our happinefs in this refpect, than that it
is confidered as an inftance of fuch ingenuity to
find out matter of difcontent, that any feeming
difcovery to that purpofe, is fure to place the man
who makes it in the rank of philofophers, as
having the penetration to fpy out a blemifh,
which, fo far from hurting, had never been
perceived by mankind. Nay this world, which is
only intended for a temporary lodging, is found
by moft men fo convenient and comfortable, that
they are well difpofed to make it their everlafting
habitation.

Nor is this to be wondered at, when we confider the nature of man, and the ample difplay of
his goodnefs which God has been pleafed to make
in the world. For if we examine that part of the
Creation, which is fubject to our obfervation, we
fhall find it filled with an infinite variety of living
creatures, every one of them amply provided for,
and all of them difcovering figns of enjoyment.
Their bodies, by the formation of them, difcovering marks of infinite power and wifdom or
contrivance, by being wonderfully adapted to their
circumftances, and fo formed as moft effectually
to preferve the life of the animal, by fecuring it
againft thofe dangers to which, by its way of life,
it is moft expofed.

Add to this, the wonderful provifion for pre-
ferving the *fpecies* of each different rank of animals in a ftated proportion : the prolific nature of

which are moſt uſeful, and liable to the greateſt
hazards, and the care taken, as it were, to curb
the propagation of the moſt ravenous and deſtructive kinds.   If lions and tygers were to breed like
rabbits, the whole earth muſt ſoon become a deſert.   The fiercer ſort of animals are a check upon
one another, and upon the other animals, otherwiſe the beaſts would have been in poſſeſſion of the
earth ; a very uſeleſs prerogative to them, though
it would have been attended with the deſtruction
of the human race.   But according to the good
and providential care of God, the different parts
of this world were kept in ſuch a ſtate as to be fit
for the cultivation of man, as he came to take
poſſeſſion of them.

Late diſcoveries have given us ſuch an inſight
into the animal œconomy and the conſtitution of
the world, that he muſt be a novice in reaſoning
who ſhould pretend to ſay, that our ignorance of
the uſe of any ſpecies of animals would even be a
ſufficient ground of ſuſpicion that it is not created
to anſwer the wiſeſt and beſt purpoſes ; becauſe
we find, that the farther we extend our inquiries,
we are able not only to diſcover admirable contrivance, even where we leaſt expected it, but are
likewiſe frequently taught to correct our preſumption for ſuſpecting a want of utility in many things
which have an unfavourable appearance at firſt
ſight.

The wonderful contrivances for preſerving the
lives of animals ; their different ſenſes for giving a
variety to their gratifications, the great pleaſure
they all take in exiſtence, as appears by the high
value they all ſet upon life and its enjoyments, to
which nothing can make them indifferent, are full
proofs that the author of their nature is a good
                                                    Being.

Being. And with regard to man, I would add, that the little attention which he pays to this very fubject, is a proof of his happinefs, as it fhews how much he is at his eafe, when he has no occafion to draw confolation to himfelf from fuch fpeculations as thefe.

Nor have we any reafon to think that the happinefs of animals is in the leaft diminifhed by the mutual aid which they lend each other: and even perhaps the very circumftance of their preying upon each other, though fo very unfavourable at firft appearance, increafes their happinefs: becaufe the apprehenfions they are in from a dread of danger, put them upon exertions, which may make their condition very different from a ftate of mifery, perhaps the very reverfe: as we often find from our own experience, that a ftate of action and danger is attended with many agreeable fenfations; and that a ftate of indolence and repofe, though fo pleafing in profpect, and fo generally coveted by all mankind, has often no fmall fhare of mifery annexed to it, and never fails to be attended with wearinefs and almoft an indifference about life. Nay, even the very painful fenfations may be regarded as adding to the pleafure of the animal, or at leaft as neceffary for the prefervation of it in health and fpirits. And this œconomy feems unavoidable, unlefs the animal were to be acted upon as a mere machine, without any principle of action within itfelf. Painful fenfations therefore ought to be looked upon as the fprings and principles of action in animals, rather than as any real evil in themfelves. But with regard to man they have a ftill higher ufe, being the chief inftruments by which we are taught morality,

rality, and brought to a proper fenfe of our condition.

Nor is it any objection againft the goodnefs of God, that he has fixed a period to the life of animals : becaufe it feems evident from the ftructure of their bodies, that their enjoyments in a great meafure end before the natural period of their lives, if they meet with no accident. Succeffive generations of animals therefore feem more likely to multiply and augment happinefs, than a continuation of the fame race of animals. Befides the care taken to propagate and keep the different kinds of animals diftinct, and to preferve any particular fpecies from being loft, prefents us with one of the moft furprifing inftances of the wifdom and goodnefs of God which it is poffible to conceive ; for many comforts and enjoyments depend upon this part of the divine œconomy : fuch as the pleafure and anxiety difcoverable in the parents of the different kinds for the prefervation of their offfpring, and the comfortable care and fupport which the young derive from thofe inftincts.

But moreover, all the animal fenfations, we may be certain, from our own experience, are inftruments of convenience, or pleafure, or of both ; and become inftruments of pain only by accident, or for the wifeft purpofes, as tending to the prefervation of the animal. Thus the fenfation of hunger, which is intolerably painful to all animals, is at the fame time one of the moft general fources of pleafure. And what is ftill more extraordinary, even the imperfect fenfes of fome animals, as the fenfe of feeing in moles, is a proof of goodnefs and contrivance, this fenfe being better fitted, from the very circumftance of its imperfection, for their way of life.

But

But the man who would impreſs upon his mind a ſtrong ſenſe of the goodneſs of God, ought to enlarge his views, and take in, as far as we can, the whole viſible creation, and conſider how much the happineſs of animals depends upon each other, and upon the inanimate parts of the creation, as this will furniſh a boundleſs diſplay of the goodneſs of the author of nature. For inſtance, what a dreadful deſert would this earth be, if not enlightened and cheriſhed by the rays of the Sun? What comfort do all animals enjoy by the agreeable returns of day and night, marking out the times for action, and the times for repoſe? The various ſeaſons of the year, contrived for producing a ſucceſſion of the things neceſſary for life and animal enjoyments, to ſay nothing of the mental pleaſure which this variety gives; the numberleſs things with which this earth is ſtored for the pleaſure and comfort and convenience of animals, ſuch as vegetables, air, and water, and the means uſed to keep up a conſtant and regular ſupply of theſe freſh and fit for uſe; all theſe, and many other things too obvious to need to be mentioned, furniſh us with the fulleſt proof, that God "openeth "his hand liberally, and ſupplieth the wants of "all his creatures."

In ſhort, ſo univerſal and extenſive is his goodneſs, that almoſt from our own experience we may affirm, that there is no part of this earth, either land or water, but what may be conſidered in ſome way or other as contributing to the happineſs of the animal creation. And the benefits which all animals, and even vegetable productions, and perhaps minerals, derive from the light and heat of the Sun, are a convincing proof how much very diſtant objects promote the happineſs of

animals,

animals, and influence the things of this world: and thus a very extensive plan becomes the immediate object of our senses. For a *Being* with power and knowledge sufficient to make this earth, and every thing in it, would have done but half his work, and must have left a wonderful but lamentable proof of his power and weakness, wisdom and folly.

Powerful and convincing as these arguments are, yet the power, wisdom, and goodness of God are still more visible, or rather more clearly to be understood by real, positive, and pertinent instances in his creation of rational creatures, who are a kind of image of himself, and partake, in some measure, of several of his attributes; especially when we compare our faculties with the means provided for their improvement. For instance, how admirably is every thing contrived in the universe for gratifying the faculties of man, and also for improving them; and on the other hand, how well are the faculties of man fitted for receiving such gratification? besides the present enjoyment, we can anticipate the future, and recollect the past, with great pleasure. What various kinds of pleasure is communicated to the mind, by the eye of a rational creature, when every thing is illuminated by the glorious light of the Sun! What sublime entertainment is afforded us by a proper exertion of our rational faculties, when employed upon the different objects to which we have access by our senses, even after we have withdrawn ourselves from the scene of action, retiring, as it were, from a material to a spiritual world! And here we exercise our thoughts, not upon the *individual* things, like the beasts, but in comparing new objects with those already known,

observing

obſerving their relations, diſcerning what they have in common, and marking in what circumſtances they differ. And to ſhew, that this uſe of our faculties is pleaſing to God; he has made wiſe and ample proviſion for ſuch an exerciſe of our reaſon. For if things had been more uniform, what a fund of amuſement and rational enquiry, and means of improving our faculties, would have been loſt: and if things had been more diverſified, by their too great variety they would have been quite unmanageable by the human mind; as they would have produced nothing but that kind of diſtraction, which prevents us from fixing our attention upon any thing. Either extreme would have produced a ſtate of idiotiſm, but this *golden mean*, which is preſerved in the preſent ſyſtem, is fitted for bringing our rational faculties to the higheſt perfection. Even the apparent evils in the phyſical world are contrived for furniſhing us with means for the proper exerciſe of our faculties. How many of our nobleſt diſcoveries would have never been attempted, had not the neceſſity of our ſituation put men upon an extraordinary exertion of their abilities? And thus the very phyſical evils of life, are a proof of the power, of the wiſdom and goodneſs of God, as having no inconſiderable ſhare in the improvement of human nature.

CHAP. VI.

Of Sin.

THUS far we have the greatest reason to be satisfied with the world, as perfectly consistent with that character of himself which God has been pleased to reveal; and worthy of being considered as the workmanship of an infinitely powerful, wise, and good Being: and the order and connexion which is kept up in the universe, shew that every thing is under the providential care of God; especially as physical evil is so easily to be accounted for, that it may be safely produced as a proof of the wisdom and goodness of the Deity.

But though we can reconcile all other natural appearances with the attributes of God, yet we cannot reconcile our own conduct and behaviour *to them:* nor do we think our actions and motives of conduct fit to be trusted with our corrupted brethren, without disguise; nor, when we examine ourselves, can we satisfy our own partial consciences. Reduced to such a situation as self-condemnation, the thoughts of our being in the presence of a God who knows our most secret devices, and who cannot behold iniquity without a detestation of the guilty person, must be peculiarly distressing, and, upon some occasions, intolerable; for in committing sin, we carefully shun the sight of our fellow-creatures, and, so far as we can, try to blind our own conscience.

We are naturally in a state of ignorance concerning the cause of this unaccountable part of our character, namely, that we should have " a

" law

" law in our members warring againſt the law of
" our minds, and leading us captive to ſin and
" death." And we, who are informed of the true
cauſe, and alſo of the remedy, are well aſſured
that this diſorder in human nature could never
be cured by ſuch efforts as men make for the improvement of their faculties, and that ſuch an undertaking was conſidered as deſperate, even in the
opinion of, angels.

However, our natural ſentiments are ſufficiently
ſtrong to impreſs us with a dread of certain pu-
niſhment for our evil actions, evil in the worſt
ſenſe, as being judged and determined to be ſo
before the partial tribunal of our own minds.
And as this world exhibits conſtant inſtances of
proſperous villainy, the natural notions of mankind carried them to a future ſtate, where every
one was to meet with that treatment which his
actions deſerved.

Other evils are alleviated, and ſometimes entirely removed, by the aſſociated abilities of mankind; but we can have no hopes of a reformation
from ſin by any ſuch means; for the more men
aſſociate together, the more vicious they become.
When they have once made the diſcovery, that
they ſtand in need of mutual allowances, it is natural to ſuppoſe that a party will ſoon be formed
ſufficient to keep each other in countenance. And
when their natural reaſon failed them, their ſuperſtition would be found a very fit inſtrument for
compleating their corruption. The heathens, in
their proſperity, are loud in their praiſes of the
goodneſs of the gods, and by making *them* par-
takers of their vices and enjoyments, they thought
themſelves ſure of eſcaping with impunity; and
even the natural notion of a future ſtate, being
                                                    left

left to be new modelled, according to the imaginations of men, became an object of terror to very
few; and when the ideas that fuggefted the per-
fuafion of the exiftence of fuch a ftate were overpowered by vicious habits, a total difbelief of fuch
a ftate would become very common.

The prefent world is a permanent thing, created
perfect, and, as it were, in full maturity; not
left like a plant or animal to grow up from a di-
minutive to a more perfect ftate : every day exhibiting the fame appearances as another, or what
little variety is difcoverable in the material world,
feems to be no more than is neceffary for keeping
up the attention of mankind. Now it would be
forming a very unworthy notion of the Supreme
Being, to imagine that he could not reform and
correct human nature, without a conftant violation
of the fixed laws of the material world; for inftance, that a ftone was not to follow the law of
gravitation, but tumble down whenever a wicked
man came in the way ; or that money fhould lofe
its nature and ufe as foon as it came into the poffeffion of the thief. This would not be to reform, .
but to deftroy. Inftead of rooting out the evil
difpofition from the mind, this would only remove
every temptation out of the way. But the trial
of true virtue is only in a ftate where temptations
are to be found. And thus the profperity of the
wicked in this world, that great ftumbling-block
to Jew and Gentile, is perfectly confiftent with the
attributes of God, and the plan of the material
world; and confequently nothing which this world
prefents to us can cure human nature of its imperfections. Proper notions of the attributes of God,
would undoubtedly free the mind from a great deal
of folly and idle fuperftition, and would certainly
                                              prepare

prepare our minds for receiving, and even expecting farther inſtruction ; but neither theſe notions,
nor a future ſtate *in idea*, could do any thing towards a reformation of human nature : ſo that
another world *in reality*, and a farther interpoſition
of the Supreme Being, are abſolutely neceſſary for
accompliſhing this great work.   But before I attempt an explanation of the ſcheme of revelation,
it will be proper to remove ſome prejudices of
education ; for we are educated, in general, upon
a tacit ſuppoſition that this world is every thing.

THE END OF THE SECOND BOOK.

B O O K

BOOK III.

*Containing an Inquiry into the Origin and
Extent of learned Prejudice ; and an Examination of the Atheistical Systems which
this Kind of Prejudice seems calculated to
support.*

CHAP. I.

The Idea of this Book.

THE reader has, no doubt, observed already,
that the same force is not here allowed to
some methods of argumentation, which the world
in general appears disposed to allow them ; and
particularly it may seem a little singular, that I
have affected nothing of demonstration. And as,
in the examination of the evidence of the Christian
Religion, I shall be obliged to deviate still farther
from the received modes of reasoning, and lay the
stress of my argument upon very different principles from those upon which the several sciences
are established, it will be necessary to explain the
reason of this innovation.

Now, as a few words would not be suffi
for this purpose, it is my intention to poin
the origin, limits, use and abuse of such argu
ments as may be properly termed scientifical ; and
from hence endeavour to shew, that it is really a
prejudice,

a prejudice, which may be called a learned prejudice, to apply ſuch reaſonings, unleſs to certain
things, and in certain circumſtances.

My plan is not to deſtroy, nor even to weaken,
the force of any method of argumentation which
mankind have invented for their uſe or improvement, but only to confine artificial reaſoning to
its proper channel, and prevent thoſe unnatural
overflowings of it, which may prove pernicious to
Religion; and which will certainly hinder reaſon
itſelf from producing the beneficial effects, which
it is naturally calculated to produce, by converting
into an inſtrument of vanity, ſophiſtry, and deſtruction, thoſe faculties which were beſtowed on
mankind for their mutual aſſiſtance, comfort, and
improvement.

The whole courſe of our lives, from the cradle
to the grave, leads us through various prejudices :
and the very means made uſe of to remove antient
prejudices, generally create new ones. Not that
this life is to be conſidered as a deluſion, or a
dream ; it is a reality, and often a ſad reality.
The miſtake conſiſts in this ; that we expect more
fruit, and a greater variety in kind, from our improvements, than the nature of things can allow
them to produce. " Do men gather grapes of
" thorns, or figs of thiſtles ?" Can the little
partial and contracted ſyſtems of human wiſdom,
regulate the extenſive plan of the redemption of
mankind ?

C H A P.

C H A P.   II.

*Of the Habits of Thinking acquired by grammatical
Study and claffical Reading.*

EDUCATION gives an acknowledged fupe-
riority : but this advantage does not arife fo
much from a more extenfive acquaintance with
things, as from a more accurate arrangement of
them, by which we have the ufe and command of
our knowledge, and a power of communicating it
to others ; and efpecially whoever has had the advantage of a regular education, is in poffeffion of
the ready faculty of enlarging his knowledge by
the habits of attention which he has formed.

The very giving names to things, if it be done
with any tolerable diftinctnefs and propriety, is a
confiderable acquifition of knowledge. But this
knowledge being neceffary and common to all
mankind, in a certain degree, would not be the
firft thing to diftinguifh and divide the world into
the two claffes of learned and unlearned : fomething more artificial was neceffary for this purpofe,
and the invention of letters furnifhed fufficient
fcope for the ingenious to diftinguifh themfelves.

Things that are natural, however ufeful or
ingenious, would never draw the attention, nor
gain the admiration of uncultivated minds ; but
to be able, by a few ftrokes, to communicate
one's own thoughts, or to difcover the thoughts
of another, by the infpection of fuch *characters,*
has fomething of that kind of wonderful in it
which has a powerful effect on the human mind ;

I   and

and the man poſſeſſed of ſuch a ſecret could not fail to draw a number of admirers after him.

The reſpect paid to this art, added to its extenſive uſe and application, made mankind exhauſt their invention and abilities in bringing it to perfection. Particularly the Greeks brought their language to ſuch a degree of perfection, and exhauſted ſo much reaſoning and ingenuity in the formation of it, that the human mind, in the preſent ſtate of affairs and opinions, hardly requires any farther cultivation, than what an accurate, grammatical knowledge of this language will give.

For we ought not ſo much to be put upon ſtoring our minds with facts, which are daily forcing themſelves upon us, as in acquiring early habits of arranging and claſſing them. The artificial man of ſociety, is neither the divine, mathematician, or artiſt, but the grammarian. Every man has thoughts, but what he finds himſelf deficient in, is a ready and accurate method of arranging them, and communicating them to others. And for this purpoſe, our plan of education is remarkably judicious; becauſe ſuch habits may be very compleatly acquired, by attending to the grammatical arrangement of words in the Greek and Latin languages, the moſt perfect, general, and unexceptionable, perhaps, in the whole *circle* of the ſciences, if we except the properties of extenſion and number.

All language is reduced to eight parts of ſpeech, and new diviſions of theſe ariſe from the different uſe and inflection of the ſeveral parts: and after this buſineſs is finiſhed, the claſſing of the words to make a ſenſe or ſentence, gives new ſcope to the ingenuity of the grammarian, and
furniſhes

furnifhes new exercife for the genius of the fcholar ; and laftly, the divifion of compofition into
profe and verfe, affords frefh exercife for this arranging faculty.   And thus it comes to pafs, that
the habits formed during a regular courfe of education, fpent upon the grammatical arrangement
of a very complicated language, are ftronger and
more extenfive than can be well imagined.   And
the firft effects of it is, that we can relifh nothing
but what appears in fome fuch regular form.   So
natural, after a time, does this appear to us, that
we are apt to confider the habits thus acquired to
be but powers that the mind was always in poffeffion of, though indeed they are in the higheft
degree artificial; and this any one may convince
himfelf to be the truth, by trying to form fuch
habits in a mind come to maturity.

A boy, who has been properly educated, leaves
fchool with his mind ftored with the principles of
all knowledge, yet loaded with prejudice, which
experience, reflection, and an extenfive intercourfe
with the world, muft correct, enlarge, and draw
out into ufe.   That his knowledge, even at that
early period, is very extenfive, muft be allowed
by every one who confiders that he has been
taught to form a very compleat fyftem of philofophy, according to the moft regular form.   The
rules of grammar are fo many principles to which
a boy is required to reduce the whole fyftem of a
language ; for this purpofe, he fearches authors
as a philofopher examines the appearances of nature, in confirmation of his principles ; he ar-
ranges the words as they occur under his different
principles, and forms in fact, or at leaft is taught
to form, a body of fcience.   And it is worth obferving, that this mighty fabric is raifed chiefly

and directly by the affiftance of the memory, a perfect faculty in our earlieft infancy : whereas it is juft the contrary in geometry, where the judgement is kept upon the ftretch, and the memory has only a fecond part to act. But when the judgement is come to maturity, it is only fuppofing his grammar loft, and the fcholar perceives in himfelf a power, and the means of forming a new one for that or any other language, and underftands perfectly how the firft grammar might have been formed. And it is now that he feels himfelf to be a philofopher. And this, though it is not generally attended to, is what gives the advantage to a man whofe mind has been prepared and cultivated by a regular education. It is not the acquiring the language in any manner, that would produce this effect ; for I am well perfuaded, that a man might fpeak both Greek and Latin like a living language, and by long habit, with propriety, yet with very little improvement to his underftanding.

It is next to be obferved, that as language is the work of man, in a certain fenfe, the arrangement or claffing of words, is a fubject perfectly fuited to his capacity, and may acquire from his hands all the perfection of which fuch a fyftem is capable. The effentials of it, indeed, fuch as that there are eight parts of fpeech, and other things of the fame kind, feem to be derived from the nature of things, or at leaft from the circumftances of men ; but as to every thing elfe, fafhion and reputation might change them at pleafure ; fo that the making a perfect language, is at leaft a thing conceivable as within the power of man : and this will neceffarily make our grammatical arrangements much more regular and con-

fiftent

fiftent than our other performances, when we attempt to methodize and reduce to fyftem fubjects of which we have lefs command : fo that a deficiency, in this refpect, is not to be afcribed to the fubject's being deficient either in truth or importance, nor does it prove any thing elfe, but only that the matter of it is not fo much in the power of man.

The Greeks were an extraordinary people in many refpects, but in none more than in their manner of writing and thinking; nor does it appear to me, from any thing I have ever feen, that any other nation had an idea of philofophical arrangement. A fyftem of geometry, not borrowed from them, I fhould confider as the greateft curiofity. All the civilized part of mankind have been content to be their imitators in the fyftem-making bufinefs; the Romans firft, and after them other nations. And thus the reading of the *claficks* forms us to a certain manner of thinking, and makes us often fix our opinions upon fubjects before we have opportunity or abilities to examine the principles upon which they are founded. They come to us in the fhape in which we have been taught to believe that truth appears; and if this be preferved, we are not very folicitous to examine whether they be fhadows or fubftance. At the fame time our tafte is formed; and without a certain order of arrangement, and a certain manner of expreffion, we are difgufted with a compofition; and, according to the nature of the fubject, are difpofed to treat it with contempt or ridicule. And thus the ftyle, fubject, and arrangement of the Scriptures come to be examined with no fmall prejudice; being fo very different from
thofe

thoſe models upon which a man of any learning has formed his thoughts and taſte.

Nobody can think that I mean to advance, that the Greeks were the only nation who reaſoned or drew conſequences. What I ſay, is this; that I could never find any reaſon to think that the other nations ever reaſoned ſyſtematically, by forming definitions, and deriving their conſe-quences, not immediately from facts, but from ſcientific principles. But this the Greeks always did, upon every ſubject that would admit of ſuch reaſoning, ſetting ſuch concluſions at leaſt upon an equal footing with matter of fact, and often adopting them in direct oppoſition to facts.

Things occur naturally to the minds of all men, in much the ſame form and order, and al-ways encumbered with more circumſtances than the particular occaſion requires, and of ſuch cir-cumſtances the moſt trifling will be crowding foremoſt. The ſeparating the neceſſary from the unneceſſary circumſtances, frees the mind from much obſcurity, and gives a ſimplicity to the ſub-ject, by removing ſuch things out of the way as tend only to perplex and bewilder the underſtand-ſtanding. And where the ſubject admits of a re-gular ſyſtematic form, the mind is made wonder-fully ſenſible of its powers, by the ready manage-ment which it thus acquires, of very complicated ſubjects. Yet the object of ſuch ſyſtems is not truth, but conſiſtency, and the end anſwered by them, is not to change the nature of things, but only to enable the mind to comprehend a greater variety of natural knowledge: and the inſtru-ments made uſe of for this purpoſe, form a kind of artificial knowledge, which very effectually di-ſtinguiſhes the learned from the illiterate; for

when

when they cannot diftinguifh themfelves by real knowledge, the learned can always filence the vulgar, or raife their admiration, by talking a different language.

But after fo much pains, which had procured fuch a creditable diftinction among mankind, the man of learning will not be eafily brought to think that, by all this tedious *apparatus*, he was not got nearer the truth, or the real caufes of things, than the vulgar, but had been only learning to arrange the different kinds of knowledge which experience, or obfervation, or reflexion might throw in his way, and to give his own thoughts a confiftent form, and bring them before . the world with more decency, gravity, and propriety, than they ramble about in his own head. But inftead of being fatisfied with fuch diftinctions and advantages, the man of learning would be difpofed to confider himfelf as capable of deciding upon every queftion which might be propofed; at leaft to think that every compofition is nonfenfe, which is not formed upon his rules: and at this pitch of conceit the man is very apt to reft, who finifhes his ftudies with his grammatical education.

In confequence of what is here faid, if any one fhould afk me, whether I difapprove of this plan of education? I anfwer; by no means, for although it neceffarily produces fuch prejudices, it is certainly the beft that could be imagined; becaufe it is better to have prejudices upon fome fubjects, than to be ignorant upon every fubject; for ignorance implies in it every kind of prejudice. To be able to think accurately upon any fubject, even if our opinions fhould have no better foundation than a confiftency with fome imaginary

ginary principles, is a confiderable point gained, and is even a ftep towards a proper examination of the truth of facts, though our opinions lead us to contradict it. For the error does not confift in having gone fo far, but in not going farther. Becaufe a little experience would foon teach us, that things really exifting are not fo much in our power as our own fancies and imaginations ; and therefore in arranging them we muft proceed upon different principles, without being furprized if our work goes on but flowly, and at laft ftands ftill, and entirely difappoints our expectations. Several failures of this fort, will bring us to a proper fenfe of our fituation and abilities, and convince us that we muft turn to facts upon moft occafions, and lay theory afide ; and inftead of pretending to be operators in the univerfe, to fit down contented with the character of rational fpectators.

I fhall finifh this chapter with taking notice of the grofs miftake of thofe who declaim againft this method of education, which they fay occafions the lofs of fo much time fpent in learning grammars and mere words, when it is fuppofed the mind might be better employed upon things. It has certainly been found by experience, that thofe have fucceeded very ill, who have fubftituted any thing elfe in place of this method. The caufe of which failure will be obvious from what has been here faid ; for inftead of being employed upon words, in the fenfe of thefe objectors, if what I have advanced be true, and if we are taught to the purpofe, we are in reality taught to philofophize and form fyftems, and (which in the eye of a philofopher is no inconfiderable fyftem) we are taught directly to make a language.

Some

Some writers, it is true, forgetting or miftaking the means of their own improvement, have attended only to the laft part of their education, or what was conducted by themfelves, and concluding that all their knowledge was derived from that, fet down the other parts, which they could not recollect with pleafure, as an ufelefs drudgery, and of courfe to be fhunned in the plan of education which they would form. We fee books written, and very well written, by people who have adopted thefe opinions; but fhew me a book written by a man educated according to fuch opinions; for that would be the only thing to the purpofe.

C H A P. III.

Of the Habits of Thinking acquired by the Study of Mathematics and Natural Philofophy.

BODIES have fituation, fize, fhape, force, and a great variety of qualities, relations, and properties, which are the immediate objects of our fenfes; but yet our fenfes are by no means qualified to give them an accurate inveftigation, even in thofe particulars which it is in our power to difcover. Our fenfes are liable to real and imaginary deceptions; a body at reft may be miftaken for a body in motion; the quality of heat may feem to one perfon to be the predominant quality in a body, when another perfon pronounces it to be cold; nay, the fame perfon may pronounce the fame water to be hot and cold, by putting both hands in it; and yet this fallacious fenfation will lead to a true conclufion, namely, that the one hand is hotter than the other. The natural measure of distance, size, and shape, is very inaccurate; and also of force and motion. Thus it comes to pass, that although the senses are the direct instruments for acquiring knowledge, especially of the natural kind, yet the philosophical examination of natural bodies requires an amazing *apparatus*, mechanical and intellectual. For this purpose, the sciences of extension and number must be perfectly understood, and still there will be great room for ingenuity in applying them as occasion may require.

The great multiplicity of objects, with which we are every where surrounded, distract the attention, and their resemblances and differences perplex, bewilder, and deceive the understanding. Thus a faculty of classing things as they resembled each other, or differed from each other, would be one of the most useful for improving and advancing human nature, above its original infirm condition. Where the resemblance was very great, the curious inquirer would have to look for some difference by which the things could be distinguished from each other; and where the difference was very visible, the philosopher's search and ingenuity would be employed in finding out resemblances. These differences and resemblances are of various kinds; a resemblance in shape, size, colour, and structure of parts, with various other differences and resemblances which are the immediate objects of our senses, such as are the foundation of the arrangements in natural history.

Or the subject of inquiry may be concerning a resemblance or difference of effects and internal qualities, which become sensible only by experiment; that is, by the application of some third

thing

thing, or elfe appear only in particular circumftances; and thefe are the foundation of the arrangements in natural philofophy.

But let us carry thefe fpeculations and operations as far as we pleafe, and dignify them with
the name of difcoveries, yet we can never properly become *operators* in the univerfe; for, after
we have done our beft, we ought to reft contented
with the humbler title of rational *fpectators*. The
proudeft philofopher will never arrive at the fkill
of making an herb or a tree, much lefs will he ever
be able to make a grub or a worm: and if he
knows more facts than another concerning their
component parts, or manner of life and generation,
he is only a more rational fpectator, but cannot
proceed a ftep towards the formation of a plant
or animal, nor advance any thing beyond experience.

Let us now fuppofe a ftudent, after finifhing his
grammatical ftudies, to enter upon thefe fpeculations, he would foon find himfelf in a new world,
and ought to be perfuaded, that if he reafoned
upon his former principles, and trufted entirely to
the internal operations of his underftanding, that
his fpeculations would be no better than dreams;
and this is, in fact, the cafe with regard to all
thofe fyftems which have been formed independent
of experiment; you fee the fchool-boy or grammarian every where, but no traces of the natural
philofopher.

Yet, being once convinced of the neceffity of a
change of fentiments, by finding that the properties and qualities of bodies are not whatever we
may be pleafed to fuppofe them, but what they
may prove to be in fact, or by experiment; the
inftruments of his former knowledge muft be laid
aſide;

afide; and his habits of attention and obfervation only made ufe of. He would find it in vain to attempt to form a new world by his obfervations of the old; as he might form a new language from his fkill in another. No affumed principles would lead him to the formation of things; but they muft be taken to pieces if we would know how they are formed. Or to have any certainty for our affumed principles, we muft have inftruments for meafuring the effects which bodies have upon one another, as far as thefe depend upon force, fituation, figure, number of parts and quantity of matter. If thefe meafures could be accurately expreffed, the inftruments would be fo far perfect, and experience would then certainly determine whether the principles affumed were really in nature. Now, all our meafurable knowledge muft be brought to the teft of immediate experiment, or examined by mathematics. The natural philofopher, therefore, muft firft of all be a mathematician. A natural philofopher, without mathematics, is a painter without eyes, and a ftatuary without hands.

The ftudy of mathematics, therefore, which is a neceffary branch of education of itfelf, becomes fo alfo from this fecondary view, that it is the only rational inftrument of philofophical inquiry, when things and their powers or effects are to be exactly meafured.

This fcience of mathematics is apt to create fome prejudices as to the nature of evidence, and the form of demonftration; which will, however, be removed in applying the fcience to any practical purpofes. For, whoever proceeds to meafure the furface of the earth, if he attempts to keep to the truth of demonftration, his fcience will be

found

found to be to no purpofe; becaufe this fcience knows no lines, but fuch as are drawn upon an even furface; and befides, thefe lines are either ftraight or uniformly and regularly crooked, according to fome few determinate rules. But unluckily for the purpofe of the man, who might be difpofed to apply the rigour of demonftration to practice, the furface of the earth is no *plane*, nor is it regularly crooked, if we fpeak of it with refpect to the fcience of geometry. Yet if we chufe to be a little humbler in our profpects and purfuits, and content ourfelves with confidering the fubject, not according to fcientific accuracy, but only as far as the neceffity or rational curiofity of mankind requires, we fhall find, that with this limitation we may be faid to be able to meafure the earth, and alfo the effects of many powers that operate in nature.

Befides curiofity and the improvement of our underftanding, our circumftances in this world force us upon fuch fpeculations, as tend to make us acquainted with the nature of things, in the material world. We find ourfelves particularly connected with the bodies which furround us; and thefe are often unmanageable and dangerous; capable of being ufed as offenfive or defenfive weapons; and may be applied, in various ways, to minifter to our convenience or neceffity. This makes it very ufeful, or even neceffary, to be pretty well acquainted with them and their natures, in as far as we may be either benefited or injured by them: and our own nature would be imperfect, if we were not capable of acquiring this degree of knowledge.

If we fet out with a refolution to difcover how a tree or a ftone is made, we fhall certainly lofe

our

our labour, but if we content ourfelves with obferving the differences and refemblances that have place among trees and ftones, we fhall be able to clafs them according to their different kinds, and thus, upon all occafions, to diftinguifh one kind of tree or ftone from another.

Now, although this kind of knowledge will not enable us to make a tree or an animal, yet it will help us to talk more diftinctly and intelligibly about them, and to have them more ready at hand to anfwer our different purpofes.

We ought to reft very well fatisfied, if thofe things, which go by the fame name, always exhibit the fame qualities or effects ; for the difcovery of this is as far as human ingenuity is able to proceed in inveftigating the nature of things, and this degree of knowledge comes up to the wants of mankind, though not to their wifhes. A comfortable *dependence,* under the government of an infinitely powerful, wife, and good Being, ought to bound all our defires ; but we are fo abfurd as to look for *independence* under the protection of the laws of matter and motion. " The fool hath faid in " his heart no God" *for him :* his corruptions are fo great, that he cannot endure the thought of being always expofed to the obfervation of a God of infinite perfections.

There are, indeed, fome inftances, where we get beyond our immediate experience. The operations of gravity are very extenfive, and very regular. One may certainly tell in what manner, and in what circumftances, a ftone will fall to the ground, and yet Newton was the firft who thought of deriving, from fuch a regular and obvious appearance, a rule for making the force of
gravity

gravity a ſtandard meaſure for determining the motion of bodies.

This diſcovery has ſubjected natural appearances more to the power of man, than all other diſcoveries put together ; that is, it has given man greater power over himſelf, by freeing the mind from a number of the moſt dangerous, and, at the ſame time, moſt ſilly prejudices. The timidity of mankind is aſtoniſhing ; we are apt to dread an enemy in every natural appearance; and in proportion as natural appearances are ſhewn to be innocent or beneficial, we gain, as it were, a triumph over nature, and in reality over our own weakneſs.

Yet it muſt be owned, that ſuch diſcoveries as theſe may indirectly create a great many new prejudices : for by overturning ſome deeply-rooted ſuperſtitions, ſuch diſcoveries will beget, in the mind of the ſuperficial ſtudent, ſome notions which he may be diſpoſed to carry beyond all bounds, by concluding that all Religion is but ſuperſtition of one kind or another, whoſe foundations may be entirely ſhaken by freſh diſcoveries. And the very report of ſuch a thing will open a glorious proſpect of independence to ſuperficial thinkers, who can expect nothing leſs than to ſee the gates of heaven and hell ſhut for ever. At leaſt thoſe who are diſpoſed to conſider material agents as the only inſtruments of divine vengeance, conſider every diſcovery as a diſarming of God. It is true, this can only be the opinion of the ſuperficial, who are incapable of making a proper eſtimate, or taking a diſtinct proſpect of the real addition that is made to their knowledge by ſuch diſcoveries.

But

But even the sober-minded will leave this study with some prejudices. Because, as the classical scholar will be constantly examining the universe by the rules of his grammar, so the natural philosopher will be trying to find out, or imagine, accurate measures for every thing. And a little misconception of this proceeding, may easily lead those, who trust to report for their information, to take up an opinion, that the laws of nature are of themselves *necessary* and sufficient for governing the universe. But it is proper, for the sake of such reasoners, to make a distinction between a law *of* nature, and a law *in* nature. And without this distinction, the first proposition in Newton's *Principia* might be made to put on a very formidable appearance, by being so interpreted as if the things there demonstrated and their consequences must follow from all possible systems of things; and that any *being*, who was to become an *operator* in the universe, must work according to these rules. But this is not true: the consequences only follow in the present system of things; for that proposition depends upon, and is derived from, the laws of motion laid down before; and these laws are derived from our experience in the present system of things, and are therefore only the consequence of the facts which occur to our daily experience and observation: and the great extent of such consequences, prove nothing more than this, that the author of such laws has, it is true, given them a connection and consistency; but it does not appear, that this is done from necessity, or according to absolute wisdom, but according to a wisdom *relative* to the state and condition of creatures capable of improvement by experience.

A state

A ftate of things is conceiveable, in which the fame fact, or the fame appearance, was never to be repeated: but mankind, according to their prefent circumftances, could not exift in fuch a ftate. Laws of nature, fixed to that degree which we find them at prefent, feem to be neceffary for enabling us to make a proper difplay of our abilities; but, inftead of underftanding them in this fenfe, which would be a means of teaching us proper notions of God and ourfelves, we are but too apt to found a prefumption of independence upon them.

What then do we learn from fuch difcoveries as Newton's? We extend our knowledge very confiderably by them: we can correct many of our former prejudices; we can clafs things more naturally and fimply. The falling of a ftone to the earth; the motions of the planets; the ebbing and the flowing of the fea, are all appearances clafled by the vulgar under different heads, and are fuppofed to proceed from different caufes, that is, are fuppofed to be regulated by different rules; whereas Newton has traced them all to the fame principle, and this principle not an imaginary one, but fuch as every one's daily experience convinces him does exift. Yet, what this principle is, any farther than that it proves its exiftence, by producing effects, and that it does produce them in fuch a particular manner, is no part of his bufinefs to determine. So that even here, where moft has been done to the purpofe, after a man of no common abilities has exerted his faculties to the utmoft, he can never raife himfelf, properly fpeaking, above the character of a fpectator. One man may have profpects more or lefs confufed than another; and one man may fee farther than another,

but

but still they differ only as spectators. A clown carried to the surface of *Jupiter*, would see the stones fall there exactly in the same manner that Newton demonstrates that they do; so that this journey would set them upon an equal footing in this respect.

CHAP. IV.

Containing some general Remarks upon this Plan of Education.

THE conclusion, therefore, to be drawn from this view of our progress in the different sciences, is this: that by means of such an education, we are better fitted for our station in the world, we are made capable of more enjoyments, and rendered less liable to accidents. And notwithstanding the frail and transitory nature of man, these advantages of education are not temporary, but permanent, as it is not a single individual, but the whole species, which may be improved: learning not only gives a character to individuals, but also to nations; for by their attention to, or ignorance and neglect of, such studies, nations are justly denominated civilized or barbarous. And as to the prejudices which we are apt to contract, the experience of the world will remove them, unless we are careless or conceited observers.

The man of attentive observation will soon perceive, that school-boys are, with great propriety, taught according to such systems, but that men of the world must act and think upon different principles. All teaching should undoubtedly be carried

6

ried on according to the fimpleft principles poffible; and for this purpofe, a liberty may be taken, of modifying things to that fimplicity which is fuited to our capacity in youth; and thus by the help of definitions we may form fyftems, by omitting every thing which is not immediately to our prefent purpofe; but it is very abfurd to think that our omitting fuch circumftances will anihilate them and all their confequences.

Language, laws, and the different forms of a commonwealth, are very much in our power to modify, with various other artificial *beings*, which men have created for themfelves; though the mifconception or mifapplication of the powers and faculties of men may be attended with the moft ferious confequences. But as to the real caufes and nature of things, it is eafy to perceive that we are not advancing any nearer them by fuch difcoveries or improvements as we are able to make, either in the rational or the natural world. We have powers and faculties fufficient for our prefent condition; but our freedom and independence, as far as we enjoy them, ought only to convince us that we are dependent upon fuch a *Being* as every wife man would chufe for his *protector*. For a careful examination of the ftate of our minds during the different ftages of our education, and the confequences which follow from the different improvements of which our faculties are capable, may lead us to conclude, that the arrangement of the prefent fyftem of things feems to have been made, in many refpects, with a view to our improvement; or if this may feem to make us of too much importance, that our faculties have been made in conformity to the nature of things. And thus the Supreme Being may be confidered considered as setting men tasks, like a teacher, to try and improve their faculties; setting things before them in such an order, that if they make a proper use of their abilities, they shall be able to make great and important discoveries, when these are compared with our powers and circumstances; but which fall away, and are to be considered as nothing, when compared with God's plans and designs. Or rather, in fact, they are nothing, unless relatively considered; it is the supposing such a creature as man to exist, that gives them their truth and importance. And to pretend to extend our knowledge beyond these bounds, shews that we are but little acquainted with the nature of our own discoveries. And yet all those who pretend that the schemes of Providence are in any respect subject to their examination and judgement, discover this ignorance; I mean, all those who speak of them in the style of criticism.

Our education is carried on upon a supposition that the things of this world are fixed, or in a regular and continual rotation; and that we have only the same things to see and do which have been seen and done before, or to rectify what our predecessors did amiss, from want of attention only, without a suspicion that there is any progress in the affairs of this world; that is, that any improvement might have happened in any one period as well as another, mankind having been always in possession of the means of this improvement: and, in this respect, the whole course of our education, and the general course of the affairs of this world, create a strong prejudice against a plan begun by God, and gradually unfolded to mankind supernaturally, and without the instrumentality of the wise men of this world:

and

and it is of the greatest importance that we should
be put upon our guard against the consequence of
this prejudice. And for this purpose, when any
thing is proposed, upon which we are to exercise
ourselves, that we may form a rational belief, we
are not to consider whether it be the work of
God *directly*, because here, in this sense, we have
no standard for examination, no determinate rule
by which we can proceed; for this purpose, all
our philosophy is in vain; we are therefore to
consider the subject only *indirectly*, and see whether it is any human imposition, which is proposed to us as coming from a supernatural origin;
and of these impositions, the more experience we
have, we are so much the better enabled to judge;
and by what we can know of man, we may be
pretty positive in our decisions concerning his
works and views.

But it is the highest absurdity, not to call it
impiety, when we pretend to apply our reason in
order to settle what plan it might be fit for the
Supreme Being to pursue with regard to mankind,
or to say what is proper or improper for him to
do. And yet this is a prejudice very natural to
the mind of man, and is not to be got the better
of, as some have imagined, by keeping men in
ignorance, but by improving their faculties; by
considering the nature and weakness of them; by
attending to the circumstances of man in this
world; and by making a proper estimate of the
different degrees of knowledge which we are capable of acquiring, and of the several ends it may
answer.

With the vulgar every thing is a matter of fact,
which is admitted upon the evidence of testimony,
as well as upon the evidence of their own senses,

with

with hardly any faculty of diftinguifhing between truth and falfhood. It is in a book, or fuch a one has faid it, is fufficient evidence for any thing. Such a fund of credulity would expofe mankind to continual impofitions.

On the other hand, the learned, with a ftrong impreffion of this weaknefs upon their minds, would wifh to determine every thing by fcientific principles, affecting to believe or difbelieve every thing as it can or cannot be reduced to fome mode of argumentation, with little regard to fact. It follows from fuch principles, your facts are nothing to the purpofe, fhew me the fallacy in the reafoning, fays the man of fcience.

The prejudices of the vulgar are corrected by learning; and the prejudices of the learned may be corrected by fober-thinking, when they come to apply their reafonings to matter of fact: thus falling back again among the vulgar, after their heads have fettled from that fermentation which the novelty of fcientific knowledge is apt to occafion.

CHAP. V.

Of Atheifm.

THE origin of ourfelves, and of the world, feems to be the moft natural, and the moft interefting queftion upon which the mind of man can employ itfelf. For befides gratifying a very natural, and a very laudable curiofity, the propriety of our conduct in all circumftances and ftations of life; our hopes and fears are to be entirely regulated by rational opinions about our

H 2   origin

origin and deftination. To be left entirely in the dark, with regard to a fubject of fuch import-ance, would be a great misfortune to a rational creature. But we are not left fo, for God has di-ftinctly and hiftorically delivered the facts to us, as fully as is neceffary for us to know, and in a manner perfectly fatisfactory to a vulgar under-ftanding; yet not in fuch a form as to pleafe the artificial underftandings of the learned. For the prejudices arifing from the modes of education which I have been explaining in this book, put all learned men upon attempts to reduce every in-quiry to fome or other of the forms according to which they have been taught. And this preju-dice is beft removed, not immediately, by urging the authority of facts, which their minds are not prepared to receive, but by giving the queftion a fair examination, according to their own philofo-phic principles; becaufe when thefe are found infufficient, every man ought fo far to get the better of his reafoning pride, as to have the mo-defty to own that he is, in this refpect, but one of the vulgar.

Being as much a friend to reafon as any one, but fully convinced, not barely, of the infuffi-ciency of it, in the folution of the prefent quef-tion, but even of the abfurdity of applying it upon this occafion, I fhall, however, in compli-ance with prejudice, examine the feveral atheiftical fuppofitions, and give them a fair trial, according to the commonly received modes of argumenta-tion, which ought to difcover the ftrength or weaknefs of fuch fuppofitions to the fatisfaction of the prefent generation, if the received forms of reafoning be adhered to.

If

If the plan and nature of things be deducible from mechanical principles, it muſt be from thoſe principles, and according to that method of rea-ſoning, adopted by thoſe philoſophers who have been moſt ſuccefsful in their inquiries into natu-ral appearances. My intention, therefore, is to examine, according to ſuch principles as have been ſo judiciouſly applied by Newton, the diffe-rent ſuppoſitions that have been made concerning the cauſe and manner of the exiſtence of things, as far as they are ſupported by experience; re-jecting only thoſe principles, which are not true, that is, which do not diſcover their exiſtence by experiment, or by their natural effects; or if they are true, and do exiſt, are neverthelefs inſufficient for explaining the appearances referred to them as effects proceeding from ſuch cauſes.

And this method muſt be obſerved, otherwiſe we do nothing but dream; becauſe it is an indiſ-penſible rule, that in aſſigning a cauſe for any thing, it muſt be ſuch as is known to produce effects, or by experiment may be made to produce effects; and is alſo ſufficient for explaining all ap-pearances referred to it as a cauſe; that is, the effects muſt be an accurate meaſure for its known operations. Thus, when it is ſaid, that gravity is the cauſe of the ebbing and flowing of the ſea, before that this can be admitted philoſophically, it muſt be ſhewn that there is ſuch a thing as gravity producing effects; and moreover that gra-vity is known to operate in ſuch a manner as to produce exactly the effect aſcribed to it, and nei-ther one greater or lefs.

In the ſame manner, it ſeems but reaſonable to require, that, if any thing be aſſigned as the cauſe of the exiſtence of the world, it muſt be ſuch a

one

one as has powers and qualities in it, capable of producing all the various effects obfervable in the univerfe. For without this precaution, we fuffer ourfelves to be deluded in a manner that difcovers greater weaknefs than the vulgar fhew when they give credit to every thing that is told them as a fact. I believe fuch a thing, becaufe it is the fuppofition of fuch a man. It would be juft as reafonable to do it, becaufe it is the dream of fuch a man.

But this kind of weaknefs is fupported by an opinion, that any hypothefis is fully, or at leaft fatisfactorily proved, by fuch an evidence as is fufficient for fupporting the credit of an hiftorical fact. But this is not true: circumftances alone are fufficient often to eftablifh the certainty of an hiftorical fact, inftances of which will readily occur to every one: whereas circumftances, if there be nothing elfe, ought always to render an hypothefis fufpicious; for the hypothefis has no feparate exiftence from the inventor, and therefore muft come from the head of the inventor in all its poffible perfection: and circumftantial proof fhews directly that its foundation is weak, this being its only fupport; and for this reafon I clafs all fuch hypothefes among the more rational kind of dreams.

Keeping thefe things in view, let us confider the different fuppofitions that have been made to account for the origin of the world. And firft, it has been faid, that a fortuitous concourfe of atoms produced every thing. Now this fuppofition labours under every poffible difficulty, and is chargeable befides with ignorance and abfurdity. For, firft, it fhifts the queftion, as if the inquiry was not about the caufe of the exiftence of things,

but

but only about the modes of their exiftence : and even here it fails, for there is no evidence that things were ever in fuch a ftate ; or even if that were to be granted, there is the fame difficulty in accounting for the motion of atoms, as of the largeft bodies ; and the thinking otherwife arifes from a childifh and vulgar prejudice : becaufe we can move a grain of fand eafier than a mountain, a child would be excufed for fuppofing the origi-nal fource of motion different in bodies of diffe-rent bulk : yet nothing is more certain than this, that a fingle grain of fand would revolve in the orbit of the moon, exactly in the fame manner that the moon herfelf does.

But there is no neceffity for talking fo philofo-phically upon the prefent occafion. For let any one read Lucretius with care, and he will be convinced that the poet is fo far from being able to compute the effects of mechanical principles, that he does not know even how to defcribe them. So that his atoms, inftead of forming fenfible and rational creatures, if they had followed his directions, they never could have formed any of the crudeft parts of matter.

This fyftem is the effort of a child to philofo-phize, upon the firft opening of its eyes, difcover-ing fomething like a capacity for thinking, but without the power, the imperfection of its organs converting every thing into prejudice. Thus we conftantly hear of up and down, perpendicular and oblique, as if thefe exifted in the nature of things, and were not entirely relative.

CHAP.

C H A P. VI.

The same subject continued.

A Second suppofition is, that a *plaftic* nature, de-figning but unintelligent, has formed every thing. And as this fuppofition pretends to be founded upon a kind of experience, it will be proper to examine how far appearances will fup-port it, or what circumftances have led men to reft contented with fuch conclufions.

Now, allowing the moft that we can to the maintainers of this opinion; nothing more is to be difcovered in this plaftic nature, than a power of continuing the fpecies of things; which is very different from accounting for their coming into being at firft, or fhewing us how this nature ac-quired thofe powers by which it is enabled to pre-ferve thefe feveral kinds. For if this defigning, unintelligent, plaftic nature has a power in itfelf to produce new kinds of things, it is impoffible that it fhould ever ftop, but it muft go on produc-ing new kinds of things without end, which is exprefly contrary to experience. For defign in the fenfe here made ufe of is inconfiftent with free agency.

But moreover there muft be as many plaftic powers, as there are different kinds of things to be produced, or more properly there muft be a plaftic power in every individual thing. And even when monfters are produced, it is only two defigning natures counteracting each others de-figns; and by their united efforts producing fome-thing directly contrary to the defigns of each,

with-

without a power to vary their defigns, and accommodate them to circumftances, fo as to make fomething new and not monftrous ; that is, fomething that can generate a new fpecies. Which proves that thefe powers are not agents, but inftruments, and that God, by permitting monfters to be produced, means to exhibit to mankind an experimental refutation of this fyftem, by fhewing what would be the confequence if thefe plaftic powers were made to act of themfelves.

However, let us fuppofe that a tree defigns to produce a tree ; an animal, or rather two animals, an animal of the fame kind ; and that a body at reft, or in motion, defigns to perfevere in its prefent ftate ; how can we be faid, by all thefe conceffions, to be come the leaft nearer our conclufion, which was to account for the origin of things ; becaufe it ftill remains to be fhewn whence thefe agents are themfelves, and whence they derived their powers, which are too vifible in their effects to fuffer us to regard them as *non-entities.*

And more efpecially it remains to be fhewn what it is that makes all thefe various, and even contrary natures or defigns, co-operate in producing a regular fyftem, every part of which tends regularly and orderly to the fame end. For allowing that the random exertion of all thefe natures, however contradictory, muft produce fomething, yet furely the man who would expect from fuch a fortuitous concourfe of defigns, fo much of life, fenfe, and rationality, which are fo liable to accidents, and n uft, according to this fuppofition, be fo much expofed ; fuch a man, I fay, would have little claim to rationality, of which he has fo inadequate a conception.

For

For even if we confider this world as a machine, it is nevertheless a machine which required an artificer, who in its formation must have proceeded according to a plan, the proper execution of which necessarily implies a perfect knowledge of the parts of which his system was to be formed, and a perfect acquaintance with the nature of his materials: that is, it required at least an intelligent *Being*, whose knowledge must be as unlimited as the materials which he has to work with; and without a creative power, it will be difficult to say where he got his materials, otherwise the materials which he had to work with, admitting the abfurd fuppofition of a *chaos*, might and would certainly counteract his defigns; which would certainly happen likewife, as they are fuppofed to have powers in themfelves, if he had not a command over their natures. This fuppofition, therefore, of a plaftic power, being alfo totally unfit for explaining the appearances of nature, is to be rejected upon the principles before laid down, becaufe even a general *plaftic* power in the earth could do nothing without the concurrence of the fun, or perhaps of the whole folar fyftem.

Indeed fuch an hypothefis could only be taken up for this reafon, that as the vulgar are naturally difpofed to believe every thing that is propofed as a fact, fo the firft fmattering in philofophy difpofes us to receive whatever comes to us in any form of reafoning. A giant fwallowing windmills, is food for a vulgar underftanding, and a philofopher, laying afide the antiquated methods of meafuring time by the fun and ftars, which were appointed by God " for figns, and for fea-" fons, and for days and years," and portioning it out with a lefs fparing hand by *ftratums of lava*,

is

is delicious entertainment for the learned, eſpecially when ſeaſoned with a little impiety. Surely
a particular providence preſided over this new inſtrument of computation, making the winds always blow with the ſame force, and in the ſame
direction, with a particular proviſion for always
keeping the ſame quantity of burning matter
within, and of earth upon the ſides of the mountain to be waſhed down by the rains which muſt always fall in the ſame proportion, and with the ſame
force, with a thouſand other ſupplies too tedious
to mention, but abſolutely neceſſary for ſetting
this new chronometer in motion.

C H A P.   VII.

The Subject continued.

BEING thus neceſſarily brought to acknowledge a deſigning intelligent cauſe, before
we can give any thing like a rational account of
the formation, or even of the preſervation of the
univerſe, we may be conſidered as having got
clear of Atheiſm and its conſequences. However,
we find authors maintaining all theſe principles,
and yet endeavouring to draw ſuch conſequences
from them, as will leave mankind (at leaſt in as
far as they are rational creatures) in much the
ſame ſituation as if there was no God. For it is
ſuppoſed, that the whole univerſe is made up of a
chain of *Beings*, the parts of which chain are all
linked together in ſuch a manner, and in ſuch an
order, as to be abſolutely neceſſary for the ſupport
of each other in that very order and manner, without the poſſibility of admitting any change: and
that this chain not only binds the things together,
but

but likewife, if it does not bind, yet it confines the author, however powerful or intelligent, fo far, at leaft, that he cannot change their order or nature, without degrading his own character, which, being perfect, fay they, any change is impoffible. Neither, according to this fuppofition, can he have any proper motive for preferring one part of his works before another; but manifefts himfelf as fully and as perfectly in a *hair* as in a *heart*; and fees, with equal indifference, *a hero perifh, and a fparrow fall*. I fhould be glad to know if any man, who has proper notions of free-agency, would not think himfelf degraded by being fo confined. But thefe opinions are the effects of fin, and fuch fpeculations are the *artificial* fig-leaves which philofophical ingenuity is fewing together to hide the nakednefs of mankind.

The misfortune is, that thefe opinions, by dropping the abfurdeft parts of Atheifm, are calculated to have great weight with thofe who are only fmatterers in philofophy, and pick up their opinions from accidental converfation and fuperficial reading. And where difcoveries and fyftems are the fubject of general difcourfe, every one is defirous to know fomething of the matter; particularly where religion is concerned; becaufe its threats are fufficient to draw the attention of every one, fo far at leaft as to make him feek for arguments to engage him heartily in a compliance with its precepts, or fuch as may induce him to difregard them. And to gratify the humour of thofe, who have reafon to wifh that religion fhould be found to be an impofition, little fyftems are formed, in which every thing difficult is omitted, and where the authors are very careful to keep out of fight whatever might occafion the

leaft

leaſt doubts: and a man has only to ſhut his eyes, and he may be perfectly ſatisfied that he comprehends the whole courſe of nature: and this we are well diſpoſed to do: for a man finds himſelf much more at his eaſe, by truſting to ſuch ſyſtems, than when he has to combat with all the ſcruples of his own conſeience, and all the imperfections of his own underſtanding; eſpecially as this buſineſs is ſo eaſy, for he has only to learn a kind of philoſophical language, and the work is done.

What we know of the prodigious ſize of the heavenly bodies, their ſplendour, ſituation, and regular motions might furniſh much moral and religious inſtruction. But without reſting where we ought, by keeping within the natural limits of the human underſtanding, even the philoſopher himſelf is often hurried out of the path of experiment, obſervation, and computation, into a region where he has nothing to do but gaze with the vulgar; and perplex his underſtanding upon infinite ſpace and time, and fatigue his mind with ſpeculations upon the operations which infinite power and infinite wiſdom may perform in theſe.

This is a true *fairy land,* as much as the imaginations of the vulgar, only we ſeparate ourſelves from them, by making a parade with the laws of nature. Every thing muſt have its laws; nor is the Supreme Being himſelf exempted from this neceſſity. During this amazement of the underſtanding, the paſſions, which never *ſlumber nor ſleep,* put in their claim for a *plenary indulgence,* as a thing of no account, where ſo much has been given, or rather this indulgence is declared to be a law of nature alſo. And to ſupport the claim, advantage has been taken of this ſtate of mind, to give us a mean opinion of human nature,

by

by rallying us upon the abfurd fuppofition that fuch a creature as man, or fuch an atom as his habitation, could be fuppofed without the moft extravagant partiality, and the moft ridiculous felf-conceit, to be, as it were, the particular care of Providence.

This is to take advantage of that natural love of order which is fo agreeable to the mind, (becaufe, without order, things would be unmanageable by fuch limited creatures) to lead us from attending to our own circumftances, and engage us in the admiration of an imaginary harmony and gradation, which, if true, would deprive us of every diftinguifhing privilege, except that of being extremely miferable, by having our nobleft faculties baffled, and left without any objects to gratify them ; becaufe the advocates for this fyftem pretend that God *acts by general, not by partial laws.* Hence their doctrine is, that if we could fee ourfelves without partiality, we have no right to confider ourfelves in any other light but only as making a part in the prefent fyftem of things, in the fame manner as the fun and moon, or any other of the parts and appendages of the univerfe, and confequently as liable to thofe accidents, and capable of receiving thofe benefits, which the general laws of the fyftem produce, without having any thing farther to hope or fear. And according to this reafoning, a refurrection of the dead would be the moft abfurd of all expectations.

This is an error that it very much concerns us to remove, or at leaft to be well affured that it is no error ; becaufe, if this be a true ftate of the cafe, our chief wifdom would be fhewn in making it our conftant maxim, " Let us eat and drink,
" for

" for to-morrow we die." For any man, with his maxin of *whatever is, is right,* might very conſiſtently anſwer to the moſt ſolid demonſtration of the exiſtence and attributes of God, *this is all very fine, and very true; but it is no concern of mine;*

> " I am but part of one ſtupendous whole,
> " Whoſe body nature is, and God the ſoul;"

and what conceit and preſumption would it be in me to expect that this great harmony and order is to be broke through on my account.

This is not the language of a man who has inquired carefully into natural appearances, but rather that of a ſuperficial novice in natural ſpeculation, who believes in the diſcoveries of others, without the leaſt acquaintance with the principles which led to them; and taking the concluſions upon truſt, draws ſome unphiloſophical conſequences from them, to humour his own diſpoſition or circumſtances; and therefore may very naturally be ſuppoſed to overlook the abilities neceſſary for making ſuch diſcoveries. Otherwiſe it muſt ſeem very ſtrange, if a man ſhould return from ſuch a noble exertion of his abilities, as the weighing the ſolar ſyſtem in a balance, with a notion that he himſelf was too contemptible to be *particularly* regarded by the great Creator, who had given ſuch proof of the contrary by beſtowing upon him faculties ſo admirably fitted for comprehending his works.

But the truth is, Newton had never the leaſt glimpſe of this chain; it was borrowed from Plato, who, for want of better information, was reduced to amuſe himſelf with ſuch reveries, and gilded over with ſome of the moſt ſolid matter of modern

diſcovery,

difcovery, by a man whofe knowledge was not the effect of regular ftudy, but gleaned up from random reading, and random converfation, among wits, buffoons, politicians, and philofophers. Such an education, joined to a lively imagination, and principles and practice which ought to make a man wifh to render Atheifm palatable to himfelf and the world, might give fome profpect of brilliancy and daring obfervation, but little of folidity or confiftency.

The dangerous tendency of fuch a fyftem as this, is undoubtedly very great to thofe who are naturally difpofed to believe only what fuits their convenience. For it leaves no morality either with God or man, and yet pretends to give an order and regularity to the affairs of the univerfe, fufficient to fatisfy thofe who are difpofed to pafs through this world with their eyes fhut.

But the order and regularity which we fee in the world, will be found, by the attentive obferver, rather a neceffary compliance with human weaknefs, which requires it, than any way directing and influencing the plans of God, which can depend upon nothing but his own will and pleafure, and leaft of all upon the foolifh imaginations of men. And a proper attention to the dignity of human nature, will go a great way to cure every one of this extravagant folly.

CHAP. VIII.

Of the Dignity of Human Nature.

IT is no doubt a lawful, and even a proper use of speculations upon the nature of things, to apply them as arguments for curing us of our pride and presumption; but if they be carried so far as to give us a mean opinion of mankind in general, the destruction of morality and religion will be the consequence, as far as it is in the power of man to destroy them. The contemplation of nature is proposed, with great propriety, as a proper exercise for making us humble, and sensible of our dependence upon God, and thankful for the great things which he has done for us: yet, that man knows but little of his own faculties, who thinks that he has reason to look upon himself as degraded by a comparison of the human species with the other parts of the creation.

Whoever finds himself in danger of falling into such an opinion, should look out for arguments to inspire him with a proper sense of the dignity of human nature, and of the perfection of which it may be capable, notwithstanding its present degeneracy: as without proper notions upon this subject, it is impossible to behave with propriety in the different relations in which we stand to our Creator and fellow-creatures, or to have our minds prepared to receive the instructions which God may condescend to give us in a supernatural way.

For if we have assumed to ourselves a rank in the creation to which we have no title, and should

I   be

be defervedly degraded below the place which we had affumed; it is an obvious confequence from this, that all our relations in which we ftand to the Creator and his works, will be changed, and a new conduct and behaviour will of courfe become our duty.

This, indeed, the infidels are fo fenfible of, that they defpair of making a man a convert to their opinions, before they have given him a mean opinion of himfelf. And for this purpofe, it is their conftant aim to debafe human nature as much as poffible, treating the hopes of immortality as a vain conceit, engendered by pride, and a ftrong prejudice in favour of our own importance. Thus it is the general practice of infidel writers to dwell upon the weakneffes and corruptions of human nature, not with a view to reform them, or even to exprefs any indignation againft them, but rather to palliate them, by infinuating flyly, that were it not for a competent fhare of hypocrify, all the world would put on the fame appearance that the worft part of it does at prefent.

And, indeed, if we give up the dignity of our nature, according to the infidel plan, all the arguments, either for natural or revealed religion, are nothing to us. For we are no more concerned with the exiftence of God, than the beafts of the field, until we have fome conviction from the fuperior excellence of the faculties that he has beftowed upon us, and the many things that are obvioufly made to be fubfervient to us, that he regards us fo particularly as to juftify us in prefuming that he has vouchfafed to govern us by laws which are neither reducible to thofe of matter and motion, nor yet to mere fenfation, which is what thefe philofophers labour to prove by arguments

ments very weak when referred to an accurate ſtandard of truth, but very powerful when addreſſed to certain paſſions and prejudices.

Although they pretend that their God is an intelligent Being, yet it is clear that he is not the God of the Pſalmiſt, who " hath made man to " have dominion over the works of his hands, " and hath put all things under his feet, all ſheep " and oxen, yea, and the beaſts of the field : the " fowl of the air, and the fiſh of the ſea, and what- " ſoever paſſeth through the paths of the ſeas."

If theſe things are facts, it is plain that the ſuppoſitions of theſe philoſophers are ſo far from being ſufficient for explaining the appearances of nature ; that the appearances of nature directly contradict them, and conſequently they are to be rejected. And how far they are facts, deſerves to be conſidered by every one who pretends to depend upon reaſon for his inſtruction, as the conſequences of this examination ought to direct the rational conduct of ſuch a one's life.

I ſhall, therefore, endeavour to ſhew, that man is endued with faculties which naturally, and in a certain ſenſe, make the whole creation ſubject to him, or ſubſervient to his purpoſes ; and that, as to what has been advanced concerning a chain of *beings* riſing in gradation, it is intirely unſupported by experience : the human race being ſo unlike every thing in this lower world, that nothing but the moſt ſenſeleſs partiality and prejudice could ever conſider man as making a link in any chain of *beings*, but as the lord of this lower world, and, under God, the diſpoſer of the things in it.

The people that I have to do with at preſent, allow of intelligence and deſign in the *firſt cauſe* of

all

all things. Matter, therefore, as such, being senseless and inanimate, and consequently incapable of enjoyment, could never have been created for its own sake, but for the convenience of some other *being* capable of enjoyment. And as the same authors will allow of no such thing as a revelation, the excellence or superiority of one kind of *being* above another, must be determined by the perfection of their different faculties. And upon this principle it will be very evident that the brute animals are created for our use, upon a comparison of our faculties with theirs.

And to begin this comparison from our birth, we may observe that man is brought into the world in a very helpless condition, compared with the other animals, who are born with the intire use of their faculties, and seem perfectly acquainted with their situation very soon after their entrance into the world. But we, on the other hand, are so much strangers to our habitation and situation in the world, and so little acquainted with the instruments that we are to work with, that it requires time and experience and care and teaching to bring our faculties to perfection; and in those instances where we are left to ourselves, it is no easy matter to find out the proper means of acquiring such knowledge as may enable us to make a proper judgement of our circumstances; and ages and generations of men have been exhausted in experiments to teach us how to turn our faculties to the best account, without discovering the extent of them. And whilst we are drawn aside by a thousand circumstances and temptations out of those paths which the experience and ingenuity of others have marked out as leading to truth and happiness; the beasts, by trusting to their sensa-

tions,

tions, without experience or teaching, act agreeably to their nature and faculties; which makes it a general law of this nature of theirs, that they have no other means of excelling one another, but in bodily ſtrength, and in the number and qualities of their organs of ſenſation : for they have literally nothing but what they have received, no talents to improve; and are as much determined in their actions by the force of their ſenſations, as the movements of a machine are determined by the weights which put it in motion. It is impoſſible for them to give up a preſent good for a future one in proſpect. It is true, theſe ſenſations do not act ſo regularly as the weights of a clock; for the ſenſes of animals, from the delicacy of their organs, are more liable to be out of order than the groſſer parts of matter. Their organs of ſenſation are no doubt oftener out of order than we may apprehend, which accidents may occaſion deviations from the original laws of their nature; but upon this account they are no more anſwerable for their actions, than a blind man is for miſſing his way. And yet deviations ariſing entirely from a change in their ſenſations, may be miſtaken by ſuperficial obſervers, for a kind of free-agency, and the effect of a kind of intellectual principle. But if we conſider this ſubject attentively, we ſhall find all appearances juſtifying us in concluding that the brute creation are connected with each other, and with the different parts of the univerſe, only by their ſenſations, and conſequently incapable either of morality or religion. One action of theirs may be more pernicious than another; but one of their actions cannot be ſaid to be better than another, in ſuch a ſenſe as that it could be ſtyled virtuous or vicious.

I 3 And

And as their paffions and affections can never be carried beyond the immediate objects of their fenfes, they can never form any bond of union among themfelves, or refolve upon any future projects, or acquire notions of relations; and this makes them incapable of what is called know-ledge; neither can they either make or acquire an artificial language. In fhort, all their powers and faculties fully prove that they have no more connection with the Supreme Being, than the in-animate parts of the creation, and particularly that a future ftate would be ufelefs to them. Every attempt to communicate knowledge to them, fur-nifhes new arguments in fupport of this opinion; for nothing can draw them from their fenfes; and if we would take off their attention from the ob-jects of one fenfe, we have no other means of doing it, but by fixing their attention upon the objects of another fenfe: for that kind of per-fuafion will not avail here, which engages the attention by the profpect of a *general*, abfent or fu-ture good.

Therefore, though there may be different and more excellent faculties enjoyed by one animal than another, yet this difference is only perceiv-able by a rational creature, and has no existence in the opinions of the creatures themfelves. They never envy the faculties of each other, nor repine at their own fituation: we cannot, therefore, with propriety confider one of them as excelling another in knowledge, but rather that they are all equally without underftanding: the feeming difference in their actions arifing entirely from the difference in their fenfations, and any change in their actions only following from a change in their fenfations.

It

It is even left to man to put their powers and faculties to their proper uſes; ſo that their excellence and defects may be conſidered rather as having place with relation to him than themſelves; which gives him a natural, and conſequently a lawful dominion over them, by applying them to the different purpoſes for which ſuch faculties are fit, being only obliged to uſe them as ſenſible creatures.

Now let us conſider, on the other hand, the nature and condition of man. Our connection with the body, is not only leſs than that of the brutes, upon our entrance into the world; but even through life we carry on our views often undiſturbed by the moſt earneſt ſolicitations of the ſenſes. And there are evident marks, as ſoon as we come into the world, that the ſoul perceives itſelf in a ſtrange habitation, and in rather unnatural circumſtances: and this one may be allowed to advance from experience, without pretending to enter into any of the opinions concerning the origin of the ſoul; for if tears and crying be any indication of uneaſineſs, the human race, at their firſt appearance in this world, exhibit the ſigns of the junction of two ſubſtances together which do not well accord, the mind at leaſt expreſſing all the marks of diſcontent then in its power.

As we advance farther in life, we are found employing ourſelves upon trifles for which no motives can be diſcovered, either from reaſon or ſenſation: ſo that the follies of the idleſt coxcomb, no leſs than the ſublime diſcoveries of a Newton, prove that we poſſeſs faculties which cannot poſſibly derive their origin from the laws of matter and motion, nor even from ſenſation, which makes it impoſſible to account for the moſt trifling and

fooliſh

foolifh actions of men, without having recourfe to fomething refiding within the body, not effentially connected with it, endued with a will and faculties of its own; and making ufe of the body and its different fenfes, often in fuch a foolifh, and often in fuch an ingenious manner, as proves fufficiently that the powers and organs of the body are only inftruments for executing its purpofes. And the fubftance endued with thefe powers and faculties, is what we call mind; and it is worth our particular notice, that this mind, inftead of being confined to obferve the laws of matter and motion, or even of fenfation, it always can, and often does act exprefly contrary to both. And even the moft foolifh ftare of an idiot, has an expreffion in it which diftinguifhes him remarkably from the brute creation, and clearly difcovers fomething labouring to work with improper inftruments.

There is a mode of moral inftruction drawn from a comparifon of the behaviour of men and beafts, much ufed by fatyrifts and writers of fables, which I can by no means approve of, as it has a tendency to debafe human nature, inftead of improving it. Neither are thefe applications juft, their faculties are fo different from ours. I am the more confident that this is the right opinion, becaufe our Saviour, who inftructs by parables, never makes ufe of this method. He never fends men to improve their morality by obferving the actions of the beafts; it would have been to offer an infult to human nature, which could not be expected from one who, though forry for its imperfections, yet has fhewn by what he did for us, that he had too high a fenfe of its dignity, to make fuch an infulting comparifon.

But

But let us conſider a little more particularly the powers and peculiarities of the human mind. And firſt, we may obſerve, that whoever attends to its operations in infancy, will be very apt to conſider the mind as equally infirm with the body, exhibiting little or nothing of thoſe powers by which one could judge of the uncommon faculties of a human ſoul. Yet no ſooner has it received, from external objects, materials to work with, than it diſplays its extraordinary powers, not only by the eagerneſs which we diſcover in ſeeking after knowledge, but alſo by the ſeveral new faculties which make their appearance ; when circumſtances call them forth into action, in order to arrange, to judge of, and communicate the knowledge which has been acquired. The different aſſociations of our notions, according to their reſemblance, contrariety, and other relations, diſcover ſurprizing abilities, and give us a great command over our own thoughts, and likewiſe over many of the things with which we are connected. For theſe aſſociations are the foundation of artificial language and written characters, by means of which we are enabled, at any diſtance of place and time, to communicate our ſentiments to each other. And thus the powers of the human mind are greateſt where it has ſeemingly no materials to work with, for language and written characters are arbitrary things : and yet certain ſounds and characters have, in a wonderful manner, the power of conveying to us diſtinctly the thoughts of others, not only when our mind is employed about material objects, but alſo when the objects are barely mental conceptions, or even nonſenſe.

This power of inventing language and writing, or even the capacity of acquiring a ſkill in them,

won-

wonderfully characterizes our *species*, and diftinguifhes us remarkably from all other animals, and,
as it were, fixes a boundary between us and them.
And yet, language and writing being common to
mankind in general, at leaft the faculty of acquiring them, we are apt to overlook their high importance, and likewife the prodigious extent of
abilities which the invention, or even communi-
cation of them difcover.

But in making an eftimate of the dignity of
human nature, they ought to be particularly confidered, efpecially as the brutes difcover no fuch
powers, or rather fhew that they are entirely without them ; and as thefe very powers are thofe by
which mankind particularly difplay their abilities.

Some brute animals may be brought to affociate
objects with fenfations, which, being naturally af-
fociated, require no fuppofition of abilities to perform it, but only to be fufceptible of habits ; but
they are totally incapable of thofe arbitrary affo-
ciations, which fo fully demonftrate the powers of
man.

Let us next obferve the faculty of memory, if
its operations were not fo familiar to us, they
would appear not only incredible to us, but even
impoffible for us to comprehend ; and according
to our ufual felf-fufficiency, we would be pro-
nouncing the very fuppofition of fuch powers an
abfurdity. For inftance, how faithfully does this
faculty reprefent paft tranfactions, a fingle veftige
of which is no where elfe to be found or feen : and
what variety of different kinds of knowledge may
the mind lay up in ftore by its means, without
producing the leaft confufion. If, indeed, we attempt to account for the operations of this faculty,
we can give no more reafon why we remember a

thing,

thing, than if we had it fuggefted to us by infpir-ation, or in any fupernatural way.

Let us next obferve the vaft powers of the imagination, which makes us, in fome refpeéts, *creators*; for by this faculty we are enabled to mould our conceptions into whatever fhape we pleafe, and thus we can make, as it were, creations of our own, and communicate diftinét ideas of them to others. And although we are naturally confined to a very fmall fpot of ground, and a fhort period of time, yet by the affiftance of the imagination, we are able to furpafs thefe narrow limits, being qualified by its powers to make our-felves, as it were, fpeétators of paft and diftant tranfaétions, throwing off, in fome meafure, the incumberances of matter.

How wonderfully is the mind furnifhed with faculties for giving us a relifh of natural and arti-ficial produétions! How forcibly are we led to improvement of every kind, by that ftrong pro-penfity which we difcover to any thing new or uncommon, and which becomes a fpur to all our inquiries! What aweful impreffions do we receive from grandeur and magnificence, and from every thing that has a tendency to infpire fublime notions! What pleafure do we receive from the beauty of colour and proportion: and how is the mind elevated and foothed with the harmony and melody of founds! But more efpecially, what a wonderful uniformity of contrivance is exhibited in the formation of man; that all minds fhould be formed fo nearly alike in their faculties, as to receive exaétly the fame notions and impreffions from the fame objeéts, and likewife from the fame exercife of the thinking faculty! And this uni-formity is fo great, that where the fubjeét has

been

been attentively confidered, and comes properly within the reach of our faculties, it requires all our ingenuity to create matter of difference, by diftinctions and ambiguous language, when our paffions or intereft feem to make a diverfity of opinions ufeful. Or elfe the difference arifes from our meddling with fubjects beyond the reach of our faculties, or applying an imaginary, though perhaps a fafhionable teft of truth.

This affords occafion, materials, and opportunity for a new faculty called reafon, to exert itfelf: whofe office it is to adjuft and regulate our notions according to the particular nature of every fubject; which produces firft a diverfity of fentiments, and, it is to be hoped, in time will produce that harmony among our opinions, which is fo agreeable to the mind.

But farther, when men come to be united together in focieties, this union gives rife to various relations, which furnifh fcope for a new fet of faculties to exert themfelves, which muft have lain dormant in the individual, for want of proper opportunities to call them forth. And thefe form what we call the moral part of our nature, at leaft it is this which gives fcope to the moral faculties to operate. And without fociety, it would have been impoffible for the acuteft underftanding to have formed any notion of them. It may be faid, indeed, that without fociety none of our faculties could exert themfelves; but this cannot be faid in the fame extenfive fenfe that it may be applied to our moral powers. And this is an important confideration: for as the mind is not limited in its capacity, it is hard to fay how far our faculties may be enlarged, and new ones brought into view, by affociating with *beings* of different orders,

orders, which intercourſe may give riſe to new relations, and new ſources of information, without
end.

Here we leave the beaſts entirely behind us, who
are not able to improve their faculties, or extend
their relations, even by the opportunities which
they have of aſſociating with mankind, who are ſo
much their ſuperiors.

The dignity of human nature even appears in
our refuſing inſtruction, as it ſhews that our improvement is not ſo much a natural conſequence
of our faculties and circumſtances, as a free act of
our own will.

Many a man has neglected to acquire ſome
branch of uſeful knowledge, for no better reaſon,
than that it was poſſeſſed in perfection by a man
whom he diſliked or deſpiſed, or becauſe ſome perſon, whoſe abilities he held in high eſtimation,
was ignorant of it. And many ſuch things, which
are real imperfections in the individual, ſerve to
characterize us and give a dignity to human nature, by raiſing it above the laws of matter and motion, and the no leſs conſtant ones of ſenſation.

But upon another account, it is of great importance to dwell upon this conſideration of our capacity for improvement; as it muſt be a very
pleaſing proſpect for ſuch creatures as we are to
look forward into futurity, which it is ſo natural
for man to do, and to imagine the improvement
which our mind may receive in the ſociety of various orders of beings; or if this may be too much
a work of fancy, it ought at leaſt to open our ears
to the revelation which God has been pleaſed to
grant us, which prejudices and worldly wiſdom
have been but too ſucceſsful in ſhutting.

And

And thus I think that proper meditations upon the dignity of human nature, according to such a plan as is here only hinted at, will convince every one that there is no foundation in nature for that hypothesis, which links the present system of things together so as to form a chain which must be destroyed if any link be broken.

The gradation among the beasts is imaginary with respect to themselves, for they are totally insensible of excellence and defect; and never compare themselves with each other, in order to derive from the comparison matter of pride or humiliation; discontent or satisfaction; nor do they discover any signs of an improving nature: an additional sense gives them no advantages of which they seem to be sensible, neither is the loss of one an occasion of repining; in short, what they possess seems to be the measure of every thing to them. And as all their excellence and defects are relative to man; this proves, in the strongest manner, that one great end of their creation was for the use of man; notwithstanding the quaint repartee;

" And man for mine replies a pamper'd goose."

THE END OF THE THIRD BOOK.

BOOK

B O O K IV.

Of the Evidence of the Chriſtian Religion.

C H A P. I.

Of Infidelity.

THE vices of the ancients were enormous, whether we conſider their cruelty or their luſts. Among them human nature was degraded, vilified, and corrupted to the laſt degree. Their very religion was contrived on purpoſe to free the mind from the natural ſtings of conſcience, by giving them a ſyſtematic method of indulging all their paſſions upon principle occaſionally, and from the example of their gods, whenever they had an opportunity. The obſervance of their religious ceremonies conſiſted only in feaſting and indulging their paſſions, without laying any reſtraint upon their lives, and conſequently could be no great hardſhip upon the votaries. And upon ſuch eaſy terms, who would not be religious. All theſe things Chriſtianity has aboliſhed, and in their ſtead has laid great reſtraints upon human nature, which produce great and viſible effects in the world.

It is true, individuals may be found now that indicate ſtrongly a difpoſition to be as cruel and

as

as vicious as the worſt of the antients. But they are obliged to ſtop ſhort, becauſe the world will not bear them out, and countenance them in their vices, nor ſuffer any thing to be done openly that greatly contradicts the genuine principles of Chriſtianity. So that however corrupted and licentious we may be as individuals in private, yet publicly, and as nations, we are Chriſtians; that is to ſay, when a man's own prejudices and paſſions do not come in the way, he is ſenſible of *the truth*, and of the improvement which the world has received from the Chriſtian Religion, though he may find " a law in his own members warring " againſt this law of his mind." And thus many an idle talker may be much more a Chriſtian than he himſelf ſuſpects; and even thoſe who af-fect (for there is ſuch affectation) to be conſidered as unbelievers, will find themſelves reſtrained by this Religion in a thouſand inſtances, and their indignation kindled againſt crimes which they would have beheld with indifference, had they not lived among Chriſtians.

The Chriſtian Religion has a firm eſtabliſhment in the world, ſo that the gates of hell cannot prevail againſt it; and if this eſtabliſhment is not general over the world, perhaps it is the intention of Providence to give it but a partial extent at firſt, though the propagation was general, that its good and powerful effects may appear more evident, from its gradually ſubduing the whole world, by the improvement and advantages which thoſe nations ſhould viſibly exhibit who profeſſed it.

It is true, we have the writings of infidels, as a ſort of direct teſtimony, from the reception that they meet with, that we are very far from being all Chriſtians. But when it is conſidered, that

6

every thing in the material world, and the whole courſe of our education, is contrived to form an opinion of the ſtability and importance of earthly things, it is not to be wondered at that a bad man ſhould be tempted to write againſt Revelation, and that there ſhould be prejudices enough in the world to encourage him to this abuſe of his talents. And yet, if ſuch writings met with a more general reception than they do at preſent, it would be ſo far from proving that we are not Chriſtians, that it ſeems to prove juſt the contrary ; and that our Chriſtianity is a yoke which is too heavy for us to bear ; which leads us to look every where for ſome decent excuſe to throw it off. Beſides, ſuch writings, inſtead of anſwering the direct intention of the authors, have produced ſomething very different, being perhaps inſtruments, though indirectly, in the hands of Providence, for ſpreading and propagating the goſpel.

Such writings have certainly been the occaſion of a more ſerious examination into the grounds of our faith ; and many a one will read an infidel book, who would never think of the Bible, or what it contains ; and thus, at leaſt, the ſubject of religion becomes more generally known than, perhaps, it would otherwiſe have been : and if the ſubject is once conſidered at all, there is no man can ſet his mind at eaſe upon a point, which, if he diſcovers any thing, he muſt ſee ſo nearly concerns himſelf, even by the reaſonings of infidels about it. For if we allow their writings the utmoſt force, they prove nothing more than this, that the Chriſtian Religion is neither diſcoverable nor ſupportable by the principles of human ſciences. But this, in my opinion, even if they make it good, is proving very little, or rather, if they

K cannot

cannot deftroy the proper foundation of Revelation, is actually proving that it comes from God,
and cannot be the work of man.

The world is amufed with every novelty, and
when the writer fhews to the grammarian, and
thofe of like prejudices, that he has tried to reduce
the Chriftian Religion to a grammatical arrangement, but finds his labour in vain, and no poffi-
bility of giving rules for every thing advanced in
it, and from thence concludes that it is falfe, all
thofe who have made this kind of arrangement
their ftandard of truth, and who, for reafons beft
known to themfelves, may wifh to be infidels, may
talk very plaufibly as fuch, though very little to
the purpofe. The mathematician, metaphyfician,
and natural philofopher, may, in like manner,
produce their refpective evidence as a ftandard,
and advance the like *well-founded* objections; all
of which may be true, and nothing to the purpofe. And yet fuch objections ferve to amufe
mankind; and, what is better even than amufe-
ment, help to keep a difagreeable truth out of their
fight.

I am no great admirer of fcientific confequences,
unlefs when formed into fyftems for teaching boys
to think accurately, nor do I expect they can
ever be carried very far, when confined to the real
truth of matter of fact, as I have explained my-
felf at large in the laft book; neverthelefs I fhall
produce an inftance, to fhew that principles which
mankind might think very certain, would lead to
ftrange conclufions, if traced to their fcientific
confequences.

It would, for inftance, be eafily granted me,
that two lines upon an even furface, no matter
whether crooked or ftraight, continually approaching

ing one another, muſt meet ſomewhere, if produced. Where is the man, unſkilled in geometry, who would think of refuſing me this reaſonable principle: and yet, by the aſſiſtance of this
principle, I ſhall undertake to overturn almoſt
every thing that has been demonſtrated in geometry. But there is no occaſion for the qualification
of an *almoſt*: by this principle I deſtroy the properties of the *aſymptotes* of the *hyperbola*, and from
them I can eaſily get at the general properties of
the *conic ſections*; and by proceeding thus, I can
overturn the whole fabric of geometry from its
very foundation, and eſtabliſh in its ſtead a ſcientific ſyſtem of abſurdity and nonſenſe, which
would be greedily received by the world, if it
could help to eaſe mankind of ſuch a reſtraint as
the Chriſtian Religion impoſes. Meditate upon
this inſtance, ye who are admirers of conſequential
reaſonings.

Theſe things are not ſaid from a diſpoſition to
undervalue human ſciences; if they can anſwer
their own ends, it is all that can be expected from
them; and the expecting more from them, ſhews
that we are not well acquainted with the nature of
them. And perhaps many of the objections to
Chriſtianity have derived their force from the attempts that have been made to give it this ſyſtematic teachable form; an objection againſt the
ſyſtematic arrangement is conſidered, however im-
improperly, as an objection againſt the thing
itſelf.

But ſyſtems are neceſſary evils, ſpringing from
the weakneſs of men. We muſt teach, if any
thing to the purpoſe, according to ſyſtem, and
where there may be improper teachers, the ſyſtem
ſhould be preſcribed. Thus it would not be

proper,

proper, where any attention was paid to the intereſts of learning, to truſt to men of very poor abilities to form a grammar for their pupils, who might be ſufficiently qualified to teach by a grammar formed by another. But if the ſubject is of general importance, and liable to be miſunderſtood, the teachers and learners ſhould be equally obliged to keep to ſome ſyſtem eſtabliſhed by public authority. Only in the caſe of religion, objections to ſuch a ſyſtem ought never to be conſidered as objections to Chriſtianity ; " let God be true, " but every man a liar."

Modern infidelity has ſomething very remarkable in it, and it muſt ſeem a very unaccountable appearance, that the more information mankind have received upon this ſubject of religion, the leſs attention they ſhould pay to it ; and eſpecially that in Chriſtian countries, men have dared more openly to ſet themſelves againſt the true God, than the heathens ever did againſt the groſſeſt of their idols. This, to a ſuperficial obſerver, might ſeem, at firſt ſight, to juſtify an opinion, that the world was become more irreligious by the propagation of Chriſtianity, which, by aboliſhing the kingdom of Satan, had even given mankind a more unbounded liberty of indulging their paſſions, than they enjoyed before : but this is ſo far from being the caſe, that the attentive obſerver will find that Chriſtianity has humanized the world ; that is, wherever it has been received has made us *men* and brethren.

Man, it is true, is the moſt timorous of all animals, as he has more ſources of fear, than any other ſenſible creature ; but by aſſociating into communities, this fear comes to be gradually diminiſhed, for every one has a much greater

con-

confidence in another than in himself, becaufe we know our own weaknefs better than that of others; and thus by mutual fupport and confidence, we are able to perform miracles of courage : and as the Chriftian Religion has deftroyed thofe number-lefs fources of fuperftition which the fears of man-kind had opened for their own torment, many now are become fo fool-hardy as to extend this courage to heaven itfelf, not indeed in the impious ftyle of making war, but by trying to hide themfelves from the fight of fuch a perfect being as God, feeking for a kind of independence under the fhel-ter of the laws of nature.

Though we naturally love perfection, and ad-mire it, yet from a confcioufnefs of our own weak-nefs, folly, and vice, we are very unwilling to put ourfelves under the infpection and direction of a perfect character. This might be proved from the hiftory and daily practice of mankind : and this makes the moft vicious chufe fate and nature, which are blind, to have dominion over them, ra-ther than God Almighty.

But this important *election* is not left to ourfelves, for God claims his dominion over us, and has given us fufficient manifeftations to this purpofe : and more particularly the Chriftian Religion is founded upon a kind of evidence which human difcoveries can never invalidate ; and this evidence befides has an extent and ftability which the principles of hu-man fciences cannot beftow.

CHAP.

C H A P.   II.

Of the Origin of the World and of Mankind.

THOSE are but ignorant pretenders to fcience, who fet out with confidering an inquiry into the origin of mankind and of the world, as a philofophic queftion: for fuch a proceeding, inftead of indicating a turn for difcovery, rather indicates that kind of weaknefs of mind, which fhews itfelf by a difpofition to work without materials; and is moft in its element when employed upon fuch dreams as the fpeculations about infinity. For all our difcoveries in the way of natural fpeculation, tend to nothing elfe, but the making obfervations on the things already formed, and claffing them either for particular ufes, which we may difcover experimentally, without knowing any thing of their real natures, or turning the obfervations which we have made to the improvement of our faculties, by giving us a ready means of becoming acquainted with things. We know that fire and air and water are powerful inftruments in nature, but we know nothing but a few of their effects; and from what we can fee, we may be pretty certain that they are not inftruments employed by God for the creation, but only for the prefervation of things; they are agents for feparating and compounding things already made, but nothing farther.

If left to ourfelves, we are, therefore, compleatly fhut out from this important information; and confequently being able to inveftigate neither our beginning or end, we muft be left in a very
imperfect

imperfect state, to die like the brutes, or at best to support our spirits with endless conjectures, derived from our natural feelings and apprehensions.

Thus far, indeed, we may be certain, from our own experience, that neither mankind, nor the other animals, are the spontaneous production of the earth, and have reason to be firmly convinced, that if all the animals were compleatly extirpated from off the face of the earth, that there are no powers in nature which could repair this loss. The probable opinion, therefore, would be, that some *Being*, equal to the task, has performed this great work, and who, as we have certain proofs that he knew when to stop, must have intelligence, and all other powers sufficient for such a work ; and farther than this conjecture we cannot pretend to go of ourselves. And we should be in endless perplexity when we came to consider what could be our reason for hiding ourselves from the sight of a *Being* of infinite perfections. Who told us that we were naked ? And whence did this nakedness proceed ?

But we have a book professing, not in the natural way of human invention, to give a true account of all these particulars. It at the same time adds many other circumstances, of which, without this history, we must have remained for ever ignorant. Now in this book it is said, that God created every thing out of nothing, and not from any pre-existing materials, nor by the ministry of second causes, but by the word of his power: and particularly, that he formed man of the dust of the earth, but that he breathed a soul into him, and gave him dominion over all the other animals; and that out of man woman was formed.

Man-

Mankind thus made, are then tried, to fee whether they are really fit for that ftate of nature which was thus formed: and it appears upon trial, that they were not: they had not their appetites fufficiently under fubjection to their reafon, confidering the temptations to which they were expofed. And therefore it feemed good to God, that they, and all their pofterity, fhould be tried in fome other ftate before they could be fit for fuch an exalted rank as was at firft intended for them. Though it is not faid but, by this trial, they may be fitted for a much more glorious ftate than that in which they were placed at firft. The hiftory of the progrefs of mankind, and of the means by which they were to be prepared for this ftate, is contained in the fame book; which is propofed to our confideration, not as a human con pofition, but is recommended to us as a divine revelation. And its contents are propofed to us as our rule of conduct, under the fevereft penalties in cafe of neglect, either in believing, or in complying with the injunctions and directions given in it.

Undoubtedly the effect which this ought to have upon the mind of every rational and ferious man, ought at leaft to be a determination to give fuch an information a ferious and rational examination. And certainly the very firft appearance of the book carries with it a very important air; for the confideration of its contents, and even a compliance with them, is propofed to us at our peril. The different writers make no apology for want of information, nor for want of abilities; which, by the bye, is a very fingular circumftance, and even without example.

Nor

Nor can we produce any rational excuſe if we neglect this important examination; we cannot pretend to excuſe ourſelves upon a ſuppoſition that we want abilities to judge of this matter; the ſubject is not made up of conſequences derived from an intricate, artificial, ſyſtematic arrangement; but conſiſts of plain matter of fact, level to the capacity of all mankind, and, which is very ſingular, is made up of facts equally intereſting to all mankind, which is a thing that cannot be ſaid of any other collection of facts. Nor is there any occaſion for our cautious and ſuſpicious temper to take the alarm, becauſe we have nothing to guard againſt but the cunning of our fellow-creatures. In ſhort, our ſatisfying ourſelves that this book is no human compoſition, or rather, to ſpeak more accurately, that it contains no human project, is, in fact, proving it to be ſupernatural or divine. Our fellow-creatures, it is true, might be diſpoſed, either from ſelfiſh conſiderations, to impoſe upon us, or merely to divert themſelves with our credulity; nay, all this has been done, and, what makes us maſters of this ſubject, the inſtances are upon record.

C H A P. III.

Of the Nature of this Subject.

BUT this account of the nature and condition of man, if true, is confeſſedly above human invention, and therefore, in a certain ſenſe, is above human comprehenſion; and is beſides a ſubject of ſuch a nature as no man, even if it had accidentally come into his head, was likely to propoſe propofe for the delufion of his fellow-creatures, as the fcheme has nothing human in its end or manner. For if the things related be taken for facts, their evidence refts entirely in faith, or in a belief of the things related upon the authority and teftimony of this book, and that in a particular fenfe, as the facts can have no collateral fupport, becaufe of their fingularity, nor do they admit of experimental proof, becaufe they can never be repeated, neither can their proof be fought for nor examined by the principles of fcience. And all thefe are ftrong marks of a fupernatural original. For if the things followed one another, according to the common courfe of human events, or might be deduced regularly and confequentially, like fcientific inferences, there feems no great difficulty in conceiving, that they are the inventions of men ; becaufe this implies fuch a natural connection, that whoever luckily got into the train of thinking, might have profecuted the fubject : for human nature has produced many inftances to this purpofe. So that to fuch as think with me, a confequential, confiftent fcheme of religion, all perfectly intelligible, and containing no difficulty, would be a very fufpicious thing, whatever might be its merits in other refpects.

But on the other hand, nonfenfe is perfectly unintelligible, and incapable of being reduced to any fcientific arrangement : and hafty reafoners are always for reducing, under this head of *nonfenfe*, whatever they cannot thus arrange. And to the majority of mankind, Newton's *Principia* is the moft nonfenfical book in the world, except perhaps the Bible.

It may be faid, muft religion be irrational ? Is there no way by which fupernatural knowledge

can

can be conveyed to mankind, agreeable to the principles of reason? If this question means, Is there no way of inferring the whole of Revelation from simple and settled principles within the reach of the human capacity; I affirm, that if there were any such, I should no longer consider it as a Revelation, but as a human discovery or plan, however ingenious I might allow that plan to be: because, whatever one man can fully comprehend, I can conceive no difficulty in supposing another to invent. But if by this question be meant, Does this subject admit of rational evidence; that is, such an evidence as a man ought to found his conviction upon? In my opinion it has stronger evidence than any subject with which I am acquainted, though not so formal as many others. But as it is not a philosophic scheme, this want of formality of evidence is immaterial: and it is only necessary to prove that it is a scheme, or in other words, as it is not suspected of worldly wisdom by our reasoners against it, we have only to clear it of the imputation of worldly folly.

It is true, all the facts taken singly, that is, if there were but one single fact must be incredible, and if either of them were to be proposed singly to mankind, every wise man ought to consider it as an imposition, unless where he was an eye-witness : for the nature of man is such, that he can propagate a single lie, however bold ; but its want of connection with any thing else, discovers the falshood, and it is but making a right use of our reason, to receive every such story with suspicion. Besides, if the facts were credible of themselves singly, they would no longer have a right to be considered as supernatural, and yet, taken all together, they may be considered as capable of producing

ducing the moſt rational conviction: the not attending to this, ſeems to me to be one of the great
cauſes of infidelity.

The ſchemes of mankind we may be perfectly
acquainted with, and can very poſitively ſpeak to
the motives of them; and may beſides, with a
very little pains, be well enough informed to cal-
culate the duration of them, and form an opinion,
from the very beginning, of what will probably
be their end.

But more particularly, there is no ſcheme of
human contrivance, but, when all the facts are
laid before us, we can account for the motives of
the actors, and the progreſs of the ſcheme. And
one very remarkable circumſtance attends all human ſchemes, that they are limited to a very
ſmall portion of time, many of them only the lie
of a day, to anſwer a particular and preſſing purpoſe: and all of them diſcover the eagerneſs of
the contriver to bring them to perfection, by forcing as much as poſſible of them into view, to engage adherents by the plauſibility of the projects:
and we always obſerve ſtrong marks of a diſpoſition to catch at the fruit of them, joined to an
anxiety about the favour and good opinion of the
world. The plans of the moſt cunning *artiſts* are
very plauſible upon the firſt appearance, and carry
an air of public-ſpiritedneſs along with them: yet,
however artfully the contrivers may endeavour to
conceal their motives, we always find ſomething
ſelfiſh at the bottom.

And another peculiarity of ſuch ſchemes is,
that if they are not brought to ſome perfection
by the firſt planners of them, we ſhall probably
hear nothing more of them. If a deſire of dominion, or even of reputation of any kind, ſpur

on a man to make an attempt to diſtinguiſh himſelf, we naturally expect even from the wiſeſt (or rather, if he acted otherwiſe, we ſhould be apt to conſider him as fooliſh) a prudent haſte to bring his
ſchemes to perfection, but particularly an unwil-
lingneſs to deliver up the execution of them to
another, when they were in a manner brought to
perfection ; but eſpecially in the diſpoſing of the
advantages of them, we ſhould look upon him as
unnatural if he did not diſcover a ſtrong partiality
to his own family and deſcendants. There is a
certain ſelfiſh vanity attending man, which contracts his ſentiments, and of courſe contracts all
his ſchemes ; inſtead of the citizen of the world,
and the general benefactor of mankind, you diſcover a creature graſping at every thing, and con-
fining his acquiſitions to the gratification of a vanity which is to ſeparate him from the reſt of the
world.

Theſe are prejudices, but they are human nature ; and what is more, in our preſent imperfect
ſtate, they are the very principles by which human ſocieties ſubſiſt, and are kept together and
improved.

C H A P. IV.

Of the Hiſtory of the Jews.

THIS hiſtory begins with a ſhort and ſimple
account of a thing far out of the reach of
all philoſophical inveſtigation ; namely, the hiſtory
of the origin of all things, and particularly of
man, with the account of a diſorder very ſoon introduced

3

troduced into this lower world by the ungovernable paſſions of mankind.

As the inhabitants had now no longer faculties ſuited to the world in which they were placed, the face of nature is made to undergo a change, that it may be fitted for their changed circumſtances. There is, therefore, according to this account, no veſtige left of what man himſelf or the world was, before the fall : and for this reaſon, there is great propriety in juſt telling us, that ſuch a change was brought about by, ſomething of which we have now no means left to enable us to form any judgement ; the only things by which we could have meaſured the truth or falſhood, or if this be too preſumptuous, by which we could comprehend what then happened, being vaniſhed and gone. And therefore the moſt regular and minute deſcription would convey juſt as much knowledge to us, as a diſſertation on colours to one born blind. It was a ſpecies of intemperance ; and to this day mankind diſcover their depravity by nothing ſo ſoon or ſo naturally, as by intemperance in eating and drinking, with its conſequences.

But if a mere human writer had invented this ſtory, how would he have taken advantage of this very circumſtance, to embeliſh it with all the ornaments of fiction, to raiſe the wonder and admiration of men ; or if he had received it as a tradition, there was ſtill great room for invention, and he could have added much of his own to extend his reputation ; and, if he had been able, he would have given it ſomething of a philoſophic air, in order to ſuit it to the taſte of the reaſoning part of mankind.

By

By this hiſtory, however, it appears, that the world was left in a ſtate rather favourable to mankind; and it ſeems the ground was not ſo compleatly curled, but that they had the means of corrupting themſelves to an intolerable degree; which there is ſome reaſon to think was left ſo to prove experimentally the impropriety and inconſiſtency of ſuch faculties with ſuch circumſtances; for before the flood, mankind had become entirely ſenſual : God, therefore, by a *deluge,* deſtroys the old world, and produces a new face of things, the paſſions and faculties of mankind being better adapted to the ſtate of nature which was then produced. And this is the only one of which we are capable of judging, being that which remains to this day, with only the changes which mankind themſelves have made.

After the deluge, mankind are diſperſed by a confuſion of languages introduced among them ; and after this we find them left to the uſe of their own faculties, which have to ſtruggle with the laws of nature, in the form of climate, ſoil, and the ungovernable nature of ſome materials which they had occaſion to uſe, according to their deſires and ſituation ; but their chief ſtruggle has been againſt the effects of their own unruly paſſions, and thoſe of their fellow-creatures.

Only we find that God takes under his immediate protection one ſingle family, and their deſcendents. But this choice, it is clear, does not proceed from partiality, but is made the means of carrying on his plan for the inſtruction and improvement of the world ; which reformation is all along conducted in ſuch a manner, that men may put in of their own as much as poſſible, and

make.

make the work, in fome meafure, appear to be their own.

It is true, we find great encomiums upon the character of that man of whom God made choice; but this fays no more than that it fuited the fcheme of God better to make ufe of a man naturally difpofed for fuch a work, than to difpofe one fupernaturally for it. Becaufe if that had been done, he could not, with any propriety, have been propofed as an example to future generations, which is very reafonably done, as the cafe ftands at prefent.

The nations which were fcattered over the face of the earth, may be confidered juft as much under the guidance of the Supreme Being, as the nation of the Jews; and when we think otherwife, it is not an effential, but a relative confideration which determines us to fuch an opinion.

The growth of the nation of the Jews, amidft an oppreffion which ought to deftroy them; the manner of gathering them together; the circumftances would make them leave the moft fertile country in the world; their march through the fea; the forty years that they wandered in the wildernefs; and their fettlement afterwards in Canaan, exhibit one continued fcene of miraculous power. And during this fpace of time, there were fuch divifions among them, as would have fhewn themfelves fooner in the detection of any fupernatural pretences, than in the manner that they did: for Korah and his company would have then found a much better objection againft Mofes and Aaron, than that they *took too much upon them*.

After their fettlement they are left more to themfelves, and the fupernatural interpofitions are only

only occaſional. They are carried away captive into other nations; ſometimes aſſiſted, and ſometimes forſaken of God: and the nearer the days of the Meſſiah approach, the more they are reduced to the ſtate of the reſt of the world.

C H A P. V.

Remarks upon this Hiſtory.

THE Jews, their opinions, and hiſtory, were matters of wonder and curious ſpeculation to the antients; but as they had not the true principles, their reaſonings about them are extremely abſurd.

. And it muſt be acknowledged, that if the whole body of the Jews had vaniſhed with the ten tribes, or, like other nations, had left no traces behind them, by which they could be diſtinguiſhed, the books of Moſes would have been a very unaccountable compoſition; and even if the hiſtorical facts had been too well authenticated to be denied, there muſt have appeared an extravagant waſte of ſupernatural power for any viſible effect which it had produced.

For, ſpeaking according to the principles of the reſt of mankind, they could never be a happy people; as they were continually in unnatural circumſtances; not being allowed to act upon the motives which commonly influence the actions of men, or even often to indulge ſuch paſſions as are reckoned innocent and natural: and theſe reſtraints were not political or partial, for the whole nation was bound by them from the higheſt to the loweſt. For even Moſes himſelf does nothing of importance

L from

from the common feelings of humanity: he has
no views of aggrandizing himfelf or his family;
nor even of finifhing the fcheme which he himfelf
had been fo long engaged in; which, in a certain
fenfe, he had begun, and faw to be fo near its
conclufion: the final execution of it, however, he
gives over to another; not in a fit of defpair, or
during a time of danger, but deliberately and
coolly: and this other perfon, to whom he delivers up his commiffion, is fo far from being a
near relation of his own, that he is not even of
the fame tribe: fo that Mofes himfelf feems perfectly to have underftood his own character and
commiffion, which was this, that he was able to
do nothing of himfelf; or rather, that he had nothing to do of himfelf, it being no fcheme or
plan of his, but one, as it were, at firft forced
upon him.

This is a very confiftent character, according to
our belief of this hiftory, but would be an abfurd
and inconceivable one, according to the fuppofition which makes the fcheme his own contrivance; and of courfe the fupernatural powers pretended on purpofe to delude the credulous multitude into a compliance with his views; if that
could be called, in any fenfe, his views, from
which he was to derive no advantage, either real
or imaginary, as mankind confider advantages. If
this be the truth, Mofes would have certainly
been the moft extraordinary impoftor that can be
conceived, not only on account of the ends which
he propofed to himfelf, and the means he made
ufe of, but alfo from the circumftances in which
he chofe to exhibit his impofitions. To make
choice of the court of a powerful monarch to
perform in; and this choice not directed by fuch
motives

motives as might be expected from the scene of action; for, in such circumstances, an impostor would certainly, at least naturally, have paid his court to the prince, instead of threatening him. And what had he to threaten him with as a mere human agent? The action would have been that of a madman.

It would have been a very bad piece of policy. in Moses, if this had been a scheme of human policy, to harden Pharaoh's heart by the stumbling-block which is thrown in his way, and which has ever since stood in the way of infidels, in beginning his supernatural exertions, with those very things which the king's subjects could imitate by slight of hand, with sufficient dexterity to deceive the multitude. But God, who has inexhaustible sources of power, might act thus with great propriety, and gradually clear the sight of the Ægyptians, and open their eyes to distinguish a true miracle; for the jugler's art consists in taking people by surprize, before they have had time to fix their attention.

But supposing all the difficulties in Ægypt overcome, (which could not have been very easy for an impostor, where the kind of imposition that he must use was brought to such perfection) and even the red sea passed; a wilderness of scorching sands would have been a strange place to chuse for exhibiting acts of leger-de-main to a hungry, thirsty, disappointed, enraged and obstinate multitude. And all this while, this very artful impostor, running all this hazard, and discovering no signs of any passion that he had to gratify, except he had been a monster of ingratitude, and did all this in return for the preservation of his

life,

life, and the advantage of an education at the court of Ægypt.

But the infidels alledge, that the whole hiſtory is improbable. They ſhould explain particularly what they mean by improbable: ſurely they would not bring down things profeſſedly ſupernatural to a natural ſtandard: if this could be done with the preſent ſubject, its credit would be entirely deſtroyed. The hiſtory has every mark of authenticity that the nature of the ſubject admits. We meet with none of the common, nay, general prejudices of mankind here. There is no boaſting of ſupernatural deſcents, in the manner of the heathens. All mankind have juſtice done them in being derived from one common ſtock, as they enjoy one common nature. We here find no attempts to palliate or conceal the defects of the people of the Jews; nay, their vices are related with a plainneſs and faithfulneſs which have given ſcandal to ſome well-meaning people, as they think ſome of them improper to be told, much more to be committed by a people ſo highly favoured of heaven.

But theſe very circumſtances anſwer a good purpoſe, and are even neceſſary to enable us to make a proper eſtimate of the character of this people, which we would be very apt to miſtake from their poſſeſſing ſuch extraordinary privileges and gifts, by ſhewing us more evidently that they were only inſtruments for a particular purpoſe; and, in all other reſpects mere men, and in many inſtances very bad men.

The interpoſitions of God have ſomething ſingularly characteriſtic; the heathen gods act entirely upon human ideas; which ſhews that they have no real exiſtence, but are only notions bred

in

in human imaginations; and in the bufinefs of the world, they fupport only a fecondary part, being introduced to affift or elevate fome favourite character; they have nothing to do on their own account, but are for ever impertinently interfering in human affairs. In the fables of the heathens, the gods are the *machines,* but it is men that act this part in the fcheme of revelation.

The hiftory of our redemption, to be read to the purpofe, muft be read with a difpofition to learn, and not with a difpofition to cavil and criticife. A human compofition we may think we have fome right to criticife, and to judge of the probability or truth of the things contained in it. But a revelation, which claims an authority more than human, and affumes a dignity, which fhews that it does not court the approbation of men, but demands their attention at their peril, ought to be received in a different manner, and its pretenfions muft be examined by a very different ftandard from human criticifm. Juft as in the material world, where we muft content ourfelves with fuch a knowledge as is fuited to our circumftances, without pretending to fay, that the crooked fhould have been made ftraight, we muft content ourfelves with alledging, that it will anfwer our purpofe as well to reafon upon a fuppofition that it is ftraight; not that this is better in the nature of things, but becaufe this fimplicity is better fuited to our faculties. And as this is what we are neceffarily led to in examining natural appearances, even where we have the moft accurate meafures that human ingenuity can invent; fo our wifeft and moft prudential fcheme will be to underftand the Bible with the fame allowances and limitations, and as nearly as we can according to the plan and

level

level of the human underftanding, as beft anfwer-
ing our purpoſes, and ſuiting our weakneſſes;
making uſe of our *natural* underſtanding as the
means of coming at a rational knowledge of the
ſubject, but watching with caution againſt the in-
truſion of our *artificial* underſtanding, which will
be forcing itſelf upon us as an inſtrument of cri-
ticiſm; rather concluding that the difficulties here
may be thrown in our way on purpoſe as a trial of
our faith, and an exerciſe of our abilities; or
perhaps as a teſt, to prove that we are of the proper teachable diſpoſition, which is not conſiſtent
with a conceit of knowledge.

If it ſhould be ſaid, how do we know, or how
can we be certain that events are ſupernatural, if
we do not uſe the utmoſt freedom in examining
them, approving or rejecting them according as
we find them to be worthy or unworthy of God?
This is, no doubt, very flattering, and very plauſible; but I ſhould be glad to know where this
teſt is to be found, by which we can determine
what is worthy or unworthy of God. Are our faculties ſufficient for this inquiry? I think they
are the fartheſt from it poſſible: and though human reaſon has been acting the plagiary, and borrowing from Revelation ever ſince the propagation
of Chriſtianity, yet it has diſcovered nothing but
its own inſufficiency. There is then no remedy
but implicit faith, if our faculties be found inſufficient for the taſk. Certainly there is; we may
uſe our reaſon to very good purpoſe upon this ſubject: for though we do not know the power and
councils of God, any farther than he chuſes to
diſcover them to us, yet it is very poſſible for us
to make ourſelves pretty well acquainted with the
powers and councils of men; and may thus come

by

by a proper and modeſt uſe of our reaſon, to form a very ſatisfactory concluſion where human impoſitions are concerned ; for the whole diſpute here is, whether this work be of God or man. But it will be neceſſary to inquire a little more particucularly into the evidence proper upon ſuch a ſubject.

C H A P. VI.

A farther Conſideration of the Kind of Evidence proper for this Subject.

THE Chriſtian Religion can neither be refuted nor defended upon the principles of thoſe narrow ſyſtems formed and ſhaped to the human faculties, which have been contrived to improve the underſtanding, by giving a regularity and order to our thoughts, and to curb the extravagant flights of the imagination, which would otherwiſe throw the affairs of this world into confuſion and diſorder.

I have explained, in the laſt book, the ends to be anſwered by ſuch ſyſtems, and the prejudices which they are likely to produce. But they all lead to a general prejudice againſt revelation, as their very end is to make men content with this world ; beſides a revelation comes in the ſuſpicious form of a work of imagination, and can expect no juſtice, where ſcientific arrangement is to judge. So that we muſt have recourſe to a different tribunal, if we would chuſe to be informed of the truth ; and whoever would lay a firm foundation for his faith, or even for his infidelity, muſt conduct himſelf upon a more extenſive plan ; and get

L. 4

into

into the wide world of things, and not confine his views within the little circle made by human science.

Even the man who begins the study of geometry, will find that he muft proceed upon very different principles from thofe according to which he had acquired his grammatical knowledge. Or if he perfisted in his error, the world would hardly compliment him fo far as to believe that the geometrical conclufions were falfe, becaufe they did not fall in with his prejudices; but they would rather fuppofe that he wanted a capacity or difpofition for attending to the proper evidence.

Here is a fcheme of religion laid before us; the queftion is not, Is it formed according to, and derived from what we call philofophical principles? But is this fcheme a human contrivance? Is it a plan of human artifice and cunning? Or is it an inftance of human extravagance and folly? The man who fets about this examination, fhould forget that he is a grammarian, mathematician, or natural philofopher, and only endeavour to keep up the character of a reafonable creature.

If the Chriftian Revelation be of human contrivance, it is a very extraordinary fcheme indeed. The life of man, nor the life of families, and, I may add, nor even the life of nations, is equal to an impofition of this kind, even were it calculated to gratify the higheft pitch of vanity of which the human heart is fufceptible. This plan begins in the obfcureft manner, confifting at firft only of promifes very remote and perfectly unintelligible, humanly fpeaking, by thofe to whom they were addreffed. The fame plan is carried on, and is continually improving, and gradually unfolding itfelf for a fpace of between five and fix thoufand years,

years, according to the testimony of the book which explains it; and for the space of three thousand, according to collateral testimony. But what is very wonderful, the different improvements do not follow consequentially or naturally, but are brought about by means and instruments totally inadequate to the purpose, as men speak and judge when they form their opinions upon the soundest reasonings and most accurate experience.

Besides, it promotes the designs of no particular men or families or nations; but takes in impartially the whole human race; and treats mankind according to their real nature, and not according to the fanciful distinctions of human vanity; always speaking to them from beginning to end in a style of authority, and, in a certain sense, in a style of contempt and pity.

Even the people to whom this scheme is first opened, and who are the ostensible instruments for carrying it on, have only faint and obscure hints given them, and such as they might set their imaginations to work upon, but could not comprehend. The Jews seem rather to be called to bear testimony to a plan that is going forward, than to be any way interested in its progress: for when it was more fully laid open, they even thought it their interest to stop it: here they make an effort of themselves, violent indeed, but ineffectual.

And the little that the prophets themselves understood of the matter, appears from what our Saviour himself says of John the Baptist, whom he declares to be equal to any of the prophets, but more ignorant of this scheme than the least informed Christian.

Man-

Mankind, however, cannot be made mere machines; and the Jews, though they underftood nothing of the real plan, formed one to themfelves. Men, in fuch circumftances, being confined to certain profpects, would be apt to draw matter of pride and confolation from them, right or wrong, whether they underftood them or not. A people particularly chofen by God would be apt to be infolent, without confidering the purpofe for which they were chofen. And this we find was actually the cafe with the Jews, who from fuch a prepoffeffion, mifunderftood the whole plan, applying every thing to the gratification of their own vanity, by concluding that this fcheme, myfterious as it was, foreboded nothing but the gratifying of their ambition in the perfons of their defcendants. And perhaps this mifconception was neceffary to make them act their part in this bufinefs with propriety, and in a natural manner, but it certainly proves that they were mere inftruments in conducting it. And their example ought to be a leffon to us againft the dangerous confequences of fuch prejudices as fpring from a conceit of our importance, when we think that we are diftinguifhed, or have diftinguifhed ourfelves from the bulk of mankind. For fuch prejudices are generally fo powerful, as to refift every kind of evidence, and to deftroy the teachable difpofition in mankind, which was what happened to the Jews. And this is particularly dangerous upon the prefent fubject; for God never condefcends to accommodate his difpenfations to the conceit and and pride of particular men.

Now, let me afk any one, who confiders this plan as an impofition upon mankind; Who is carrying it on? It cannot be the Jews, for they know

know nothing of the matter; and when the strength of its evidence awaked them from their ambitious dream, they set themselves violently to oppose it.

It may, however, be pretended, that schemes have extended themselves by natural means, and have received gradual improvements from one age to another, without any intention to bring them to what they have accidentally arrived; the improvements being only the natural consequence of the operations of the faculties of men in certain circumstances. This, for instance, is generally the case with the improvements in science: and why, it may be said, may not religion have proceeded and improved by the same means?

But we must observe, that the most intricate sciences appear no longer mysterious after they are discovered: And this is so much a truth, that we can hardly conceive a person, with a proper use of his faculties, and these properly prepared, to have been in the same circumstances, and in the same train of thinking, without making the same discovery. And all mankind, who are capable of understanding any discoveries in science, may be conceived in circumstances which would infallibly have led them to make the discoveries themselves. Every one who knows any thing of arts and sciences, must feel himself so much at his ease upon such subjects, that he would never think of referring the discovery of them to a supernatural power. Besides, the first steps in any science are perfectly clear and intelligible, and always the easiest to be understood; they are only deficient in extent and *generality.*

But this is so far from being the case with our religion, that it is all darkness till we come to
the

the times of our Saviour; and if he had never come, the whole would have been nothing: but this is not the cafe with human improvements and projects; they are always fomething, as far as they go; and the fuppofing them to ftop at any part, will exhibit a certain degree of perfection, and afford a leffon to mankind either of what they are to follow or fhun. But if the Chriftian fcheme had ftopt fhort, no ufe could have been made of it by man; for there is no probability that any body would think of threatening and terrifying a king by plagues and miracles, and then proceed to carry off the moft laborious of his fubjects, leading them through an arm of the fea, and keeping them forty years in a wildernefs to be fed and cloathed miraculoufly. In fhort, mankind can neither imitate, nor apply to any worldly purpofe, any part of this plan.

It has been faid, though by very weak people indeed, that the whole is a fiction, refembling the extravagance of romance: but it has produced too many confequences in the world to allow any one to dwell a moment upon fuch a fuppofition: and what is immediately to our purpofe, we have ample proof of what mankind have been able to do upon religious fubjects, when left to themfelves, and to their own inventions; and by the fpecimens that they have given us, we fee that their inventions are poor indeed.

Romances are always the invention of one head, and the actors are obvioufly imaginary *beings*, adorned with an appearance of fupernatural power, and yet employed in nothing but bringing about human events in a very unnatural manner. But in the Bible, fupernatural events are brought about by the inftrumentality of mere men; and even the part that our Saviour himfelf has to tranf-
act,

act, he performs in the person of a man. The nature of fabulous compositions is so well understood, that it may be reduced to rules: And I can form as determinate a judgement upon reading a romance, as when I examine the solution of an algebraic problem.

Does any body believe in the existence of the actors in fables? Does any one doubt of the existence of the nation of the Jews; or of the existence of the Christians, who have been the instruments in conducting this plan since it was taken out of their hands? Believe as little as you please upon this subject; no man of common sense can help believing so much as will support the opinion that a plan has been carrying on. And although it be conducted according to the principles of no human sciences or compositions, this is no argument of its want of proof, but only conveys to us this necessary information, that we must become as *little children*, laying aside our scientific prejudices, which tend to destroy the teachable disposition in us, and prepare ourselves for learning a new science founded upon new evidence.

C H A P. VII.

Of the Nature of this Plan.

WHEN we discover a scheme begun in the remotest ages, and which has been every day opening and enlarging itself, not according to the plan of human discoveries, but by methods singular and impossible to human ingenuity to contrive, or rather, which in human hands would have produced no effect, it becomes absolutely

neceſſary to go beyond this world for the author
and conductor of ſuch a work.

Even the human agents who have their parts to
act in it, do not engage in them like men profe-
cuting their own views, but they have ſomething
of an appearance of being forced into the ſervice,
or at leaſt like a man waiting for, and acting by,
the direction of a maſter: ſo much does every
thing put on a ſupernatural air.

Such a ſcheme would be worthy of the attention
of a philoſopher in the higheſt degree, as a matter
of mere curioſity. But when it is of the moſt intereſting nature to man, as ſetting life and death
before him in the higheſt ſenſe of thoſe words,
this ſcheme ought to be conſidered, in a certain
ſenſe, as every thing: and if the book does really
unfold it, all other circumſtances are to be ſet
aſide: criticiſms founded upon our ſyſtematic
modes of arrangement, or upon our forms of expreſſion, are trifling and impertinent, ſpeaking
with no more reverence than we do of human
compoſitions. But when we conſider ourſelves
and the ſubject, and the author of the plan, ſuch
a conduct is to the laſt degree hazardous and abſurd
and impious *.

The natural world is a ſcheme or ſyſtem of
which we may comprehend enough to anſwer our

---

* Even a man of abilities may ſpeak with contempt of
the impertinent criticiſms made upon his works by a weak
man: thus there ſeems no impropriety in Monteſquieu's
ſaying, " A l'égard du plan que le petit miniſtre de Wit-
" temberg voudroit que j'euſſe ſuivi dans un ouvrage qui
" porte le titre d'*Eſprit des lois* repondez-lui que mon in-
" tention a été de faire mon ouvrage, et non pas le ſien."
But language cannot convey the contempt that any man deſerves who would pretend to direct God Almighty.

neceſſary purpoſes, beſides furniſhing matter to exerciſe our reaſon and ingenuity upon. Yet when
we would attempt to comprehend every thing,
we ſoon meet with ſuch difficulties as ought to
make us ſenſible of our ſhort-ſightedneſs. But
inſtead of learning ſuch an uſeful leſſon, the The-
oriſt is diſpoſed to conſider whatever occaſions ſuch
difficulties, as foreign to the purpoſe, and would
have been much better pleaſed with a world
formed according to ſome hypotheſis of his own.

In the ſame manner our theoretical moraliſts,
pretend to find inſurmountable difficulties in the
Bible, much matter that will not fall in with their
ſchemes, and therefore, as they pretend, foreign
to the purpoſe; much of the ſtyle and arrangement not reducible to the generally received modes
of compoſition, and therefore abſurd.

But the courſe of nature, and the courſe of religion, keep on their ſtated grogreſs; and with
an awful indifference ſeem to be telling ſuch objectors, that it is the intention of God to execute
his own plan, and not theirs.

We are taught by God that he made mankind
and every thing elſe, not by laws, or according to
any eſtabliſhed neceſſary courſe of things: that
is, there was nothing done at that time, which, if
it were done again, we have any reaſon to think
would produce the ſame effect by way of natural
conſequence. Laws of nature, then, are poſterior
to the creation, and conſequently depending upon
the will of God. But mankind always proceed
upon the abſurd ſuppoſition, that the laws which
preſerve things in being, made them at firſt, which
ſhews that the idea of a creation is not a human
idea. Man, and we have no reaſon to think
otherwiſe of the whole animal creation, was formed
contrary

contrary to the laws of nature; inftead of a gradual progrefs from infancy to maturity, he is
made perfect at once. After this, the laws of
nature commence: that is, inftead of a fucceffion
of continually varying objects; things either remain invariably the fame, or generations of men,
plants, and animals, fucceed each other according
to a ftated rule; or, after a time, the fame objects are exhibited again in the fame circumftances.
All thefe appearances form habits in us. And
upon thefe, taken in the moft extenfive fenfe, all
our improvement, as rational creatures, depends.
But fome people are fo abfurd as to think that our
very mind depends upon them, and is only a compofition of fuch habits. What a human mind
would be without the knowledge that it receives
from fenfation and reflection, it is impoffible for
us to fay, though it feems but reafonable to fuppofe, that the knowledge which we are capable of
acquiring at prefent depends upon the will of God,
and is not a neceffary confequence of any laws of
nature. The Scripture makes the formation of
the foul and body two diftinct acts of God, and
the compofition of which they are made, two diftinct fubftances; the one is called the duft of the
earth, the other the breath of God.

But to quicken our attention to the laws of nature, which God had eftablifhed, and haften our
improvement, we are put into a ftate of trial and
temptation; things may be properly ufed or
abufed by us; pleafure and pain are annexed to
the application of certain things, often not immediate but confequential, and in fome diftant period of time, on purpofe to engage us to look
forward into futurity.

What

What the firſt laws of nature were with reſpect to man, is not ſaid in the Bible, only it appears, upon trial, that human nature, even in its perfect ſtate, was not equal to the temptations to which it might be expoſed, and a particular event ſeemed to have compleated the ruin of mankind ; and, if left to themſelves, they muſt have gone on propagating a race naturally devoted to eternal damnation ; which ſtate the Scripture, as it calls natural death ſleep, calls eternal death.

Inſtead of creating a new race of men, who might ſtand in need of no reformation, God makes, as it were, a new creation with regard to man, curſes the ground, and thus begins the reformation of the race, which had degenerated ; and this reformation will undoubtedly be carried on and compleated in a way which, in the end, will ſet his power, wiſdom, and goodneſs in the ſtrongeſt light that man, or perhaps angels, can behold them.

His plan, as we may collect it from what he has been pleaſed to diſcover, ſeems to be this ; to make mankind as much as poſſible the inſtruments of their own reformation, only helping them on, where it was impoſſible for them to do without help. Thus condeſcending to be the teacher of mankind, and ſuiting his leſſons to their capacities, faculties, and circumſtances, as a ſchoolmaſter would try and exerciſe and improve the capacities and faculties of his ſcholars. And to keep to the ſame figure, if I were to teach a boy ſomething directly, which I knew his abilities could not reach of themſelves ; but with regard to another, only put him into circumſtances, where he could not fail to learn of himſelf what he wanted, if he made the proper uſe of his faculties ;

M

ties; the firſt would confider himſelf as obliged to me for his inſtruction; whereas the ſecond would aſcribe the knowledge which he had acquired entirely to himſelf.

In the ſame manner God is condeſcending to teach us in two different ways; in the natural, he has put fixed laws before us, which we may examine; and improve by the examination, if we attend to their regular and ſtated conſequences; and theſe are well proportioned to, the length of our lives. If the annual courſe of the ſun had only been an hundred times as great as at preſent, no man could have experienced the variety of the four ſeaſons.

On the other hand, in the ſupernatural world God has condeſcended to diſcover to us what, of ourſelves, we never could have found out; however, not in ſuch a manner as to encourage our indolence, but encumbered with ſuch difficulties as require a very conſiderable, and, at the ſame time, a very prudent exertion of our faculties, to turn to proper account.

Even the matters of fact are myſterious; they do not follow ſtated laws, like thoſe to which ſuch events as are proportioned to the life and faculties of man are ſubject. The life of the world is only the regular period of them; ſo that new worlds, like new years, muſt paſs away, before any principles for eſtabliſhing laws could be found; and therefore our conviction cannot, upon ſuch ſubjects, be grounded in habit, but in faith.

In the material world, the regular returns of certain appearances, that are variable to a certain degree, and the qualities and properties of matter being fixed, all theſe form very ſtrong habits; their frequent appearance, and the conſtant opportunities.

tunities which we have of examining them, wear off all air of myſtery in natural things, and a familiarity with them we miſtake for an acquaintance with their natures: and although we ſee only the conſtant effects and regular appearances, yet we find this a knowledge that gives us great ſatisfaction, and we are apt to conclude, that the foundation of ſuch appearances is immoveable, though we cannot tell what it is. And thoſe who confine their views to this world, labour only to make their circumſtances and expectations conſiſtent with each other.

But, on the other hand, though the things in the ſpiritual world are no more myſterious than in the material, yet no habits of this kind can be formed; we have only a ſucceſſion of appearances, all different, and which we are only told tend to a very remote, though a very important end: and how they are means to bring about that end, we cannot tell; and therefore the myſterious air can never forſake even the matters of fact, and we have nothing for it, but to put an entire faith and confidence in God, not that he is carrying on ſuch a ſcheme, for we have ſufficient natural evidence for that, but that he will bring it to perfection in the way which he has promiſed, and that we ourſelves are as much intereſted in it, as it is ſaid in the Bible that we are; and as the event can only give us the natural conviction upon theſe points, their evidence muſt, at preſent, be the evidence of faith.

Yet even this ſpiritual plan, is made as level as poſſible, at leaſt as level as neceſſary to our capacities, by being, in a great meaſure, put into the hands of human actors; and brought forward, not ſilently and ſuddenly, ſo as to eſcape our obſerva-

tion,

vation, but with such a gradual oppofition from
worldly-minded men, as could not retard its progrefs, yet was fufficient to draw the attention of
mankind, and keep them fenfible that fuch a
fcheme was going forward.

And for this purpofe, it firft of all pleafed God
to make the two grand divifions of the world into
Jew and Gentile: and though the Jews feem more
immediately under the protection of God, yet we
have no reafon to look upon the heathen part as
neglected; and a man would judge very errone-
oufly, who fhould afcribe God's dealings with the
Jews to partiality, or to think that this conduct
exhibited him in the character of a refpecter of
perfons.   For, upon a nearer infpection, it will be
found that God does not fo properly protect the
Jews as his own fcheme; becaufe the feparation of
the Jews from the reft of the world, was not intended as the means of making them a flourifhing
nation, but only to preferve the worfhip of the
true God, and proper notions of his attributes,
and to be fuch a proof as all mankind could comprehend, that God was carrying on this plan of
religion; at the fame time that the reft of the
world, in all variety of circumftances, were to exhibit what human nature is of itfelf, and what it
is *capable* of doing, and *able* to do, when left to itfelf.   And thus, by a comparifon of all circumftances, the rational and teachable part of the
world, in the fulnefs of time would be able to
ground their faith upon the foundeft reafonings.

This view of the fubject accounts very fully
for God's fuffering the greateft part of mankind,
for fo long a time, *to walk after their own ways*;
and it will alfo have a tendency to moderate the
very high opinion which we are apt to form of
                                                    fuper-

supernatural endowments, by making us put a value upon them according to the circumstances of
the man who receives them, and not according to
the excellence of the endowments themselves,
which is what we are naturally disposed to do.
For a man who has nothing but what he has received, may be as weak and frail, though en-
trusted to work miracles upon occasion, as another whom the Supreme Being only puts in proper
circumstances to exert what are considered as his
natural powers.

If this plan had been the work of men, their
tampering with it would have soon discovered its
nature: for when objections of any seeming consequence had been made, those who thought themselves interested in its preservation, would have
been trying to accommodate it to every new hypothesis, and this must have exposed its *human* foundation to the eyes of the whole world. And I
suppose, that the well-wishers to religion, in every
age, have heard objections against it, which they
could have wished to see properly refuted, and
when that could not be done, even that the very
occasion of them had been taken away. Whence
this great respect for an imposition? And why
this fear of meddling with the works of their
own hands? Or rather, does not this prove beyond contradiction, that it is a supernatural work;
the very stumbling-blocks in it, having too awful
an appearance to be touched with sacrilegious
hands?

God's plan seems to be the same in his natural,
and in what, for distinction's sake, we call his supernatural dispensations: we may destroy or neglect the proper means for our bodily preservation,
by not paying a sufficient attention to the laws of

nature

nature ; in the fame manner, our fpiritual welfare is entrufted to our own care. We have a part affigned us to act, and we are put into certain cir-cumftances, and find that we have fo much power over ourfelves, and the nature of things, that we are the firft to blame ourfelves for a neglect of our duty in any refpect. We find ourfelves con-ducted, but not compelled. All things exhibit the appearance of an improving nature in man, and this, not from neceffity, but voluntarily, as appears by the neglect of too many. And this improvement, we have reafon to hope, may 'be carried to a degree which is hardly conceivable in fuch limited, corrupted, and dependent creatures, by God's interpofition, according to the plan of Chriftianity.

What a leffon will the general judgement afford to the well-difpofed, when the fecrets of all hearts fhall be laid open! Sufficient, we may fuppofe, to preferve the new world from fuch a fatal accident as happened to this.

The more fuch a plan as this is put into the hands of men, and, where that may be impoffible, the more it is made to pafs through the hands of men, the more likely it appears to be to anfwer the ends which the Supreme Being feems to have in view, namely, that of perfecting human nature by the operations of men, in one fenfe or ano-ther.

CHAP. VIII.

Of the Character of Christ.

IF what has been said in the last chapter be properly confidered, the appearance of the Son of God in the perfon and character of a man, will be found neither improper nor unneceffary. To confirm this, let us take a view of his character and behaviour whilst among men. But here we shall err egregioufly, if we pretend to judge of his conduct according to thofe rules by which mankind are influenced and governed, on the one hand; or on the other, by thofe according to which we judge of the attributes of God; thefe are the two extremes which ought to be avoided.

The proper light to view him in, is that of a perfon acting a part affigned him, or here more properly a part which he has been pleafed to take up; neglecting his own natural powers, or concealing them to accommodate himfelf to the character which he had undertaken to reprefent. And thus it muft become a part of his character to conceal his powers, except in as far as was neceffary for the work which he had to perform. His character is not to be tried by the attributes of God. It is to be tried by the circumftances of mankind, and the nature of his office; and if this affumed character be fuited to thefe, his divinity is by no means affected by it. And, if the dignity of the fubject was not above all comparifon, I would add, no more than the wifdom of a man could be called in queftion, becaufe he had reprefented to advantage the character of a fool.

This

This feems to me to account very fully for the great caution ufed by our Saviour to conceal himfelf from the people, in every circumftance which might difcover him to be the Meffiah, except thofe which could be collected from his foretold character; not, I think, as Locke fays, that he was afraid to difcover himfelf before the time; for his prophetic character feems to me to be what he wants to difcover himfelf by, and he wants the inference to be made from this character; and this is the reafon why it is faid fuch a thing was done that the Scriptures might be fulfilled; as if he had no other motive for doing thofe things, but only to furnifh the confiderate and attentive reafoner with full evidence, that *his* was no new fcheme, but that he was carrying on the fcheme delivered in the Old Teftament; or, to ufe his own expreffion, that he was not come to deftroy the law and the prophets, but to fulfil them.

And if he had appeared in any other character, and exerted the moft amazing powers in wonders and miracles of every kind daily, he might have forced a reception of himfeif upon mankind, for whatever he pleafed; but he never could have been confidered as carrying on the Jewifh fcheme, which had been begun fo many ages before, and bringing it to perfection: and his miracles, had they been never fo numerous, could not have produced fo ftrong an argument as we have at prefent, nor would the conviction have been fo rational, as that which is forced upon the mind from a long connected plan, carried on through the whole of time, and which we have good reafon to conclude will only ceafe with time. Such a connected plan removes all fufpicion of any temporary

rary

rary deluſion, to which it might be pretended a whole nation might be ſubject occaſionally.

His whole character, indeed, is the moſt wonderful that can be conceived, every circumſtance of it manifeſting the commiſſion which he had undertaken. If he had exhibited more or leſs power, it could not have anſwered his purpoſe ſo well. His prophetic character is contradictory to the principles of human nature, but is accurately preſerved by him. His ſtation in the world was ſuch as is looked upon with contempt. But he who knew ſo well what was in man, knew alſo that the difference was immaterial whether he acted the king or the beggar.

Even a mind properly tutored by philoſophy, comes to acknowledge the vanity of all human diſtinctions; though it cannot arrive at ſuch perfection as to be above being influenced by them. And thus we may eaſily conceive, that the moſt ſplendid of human titles would have been particularly degrading to the Son of God. It was wonderful condeſcenſion to take our nature upon him, without the humiliating circumſtance of being ſtill farther encumbered with our vanities.

I ſhall conclude, with obſerving the extraordinary teſtimony which he has left us of the innocence of his character, by chuſing, as his conſtant companion, and witneſs of all his actions, the worſt man, we may ſuppoſe, that ever this world produced, who was preſent with him in public and private, and who would have been forward enough to produce any thing that could have been laid to his charge.

CHAP.

C H A P. IX.

Of the Miracles of Chrift.

TO the careful obferver, and unprejudiced reafoner, even the lefs obvious circumftances of
our Saviour's character and behaviour will carry
irrefiftible conviction along with them ; though to
the dull apprehenfions of thofe who cannot go a
ftep beyond the immediate objects of their fenfes,
miracles were neceffary ; and not only neceffary
for this reafon, but alfo becaufe they make a part
of our Saviour's character, that he was the Son of
God with power.

But even thefe are not merely wonderful works ;
for whoever confiders his miracles with attention,
muft acknowledge, if he knows any thing of human nature, that the very felection of them is by
no means fo very obvious. They are not of the
kind which an impoftor could or would try to put
upon mankind ; and indeed they are of fuch a
kind as he could not poffibly fucceed in, among
the moft credulous people. Though they appear
to be great and truly fupernatural when confidered
attentively, yet they are not fuch as have a ten--
dency to raife the wonder and admiration of a
multitude. No fhowy miracles are performed,
nor fuch as are calculated to dazzle and alarm
mankind. Difeafes are healed, and, in one inftance, the dead is raifed, which was certainly done
to fupport his character, as he profeffed to have
power to raife the dead ; for in his anfwer to the
difciples

diſciples of John the Baptiſt, the dead being raiſed is a circumſtance mentioned.

All his miracles are more than barely ſupernatural wonders; they have beſides their ſupernatural character, a particular application to our Saviour's character and miſſion; and cannot be fully underſtood, unleſs this circumſtance be properly attended to. They were not merely neceſſary to gain credit to him as a ſupernatural teacher, for they muſt be conſidered in relation to the plan which was carrying on, if we would ſee them in their full force.

The objections made to miracles in general, are nothing to the purpoſe. For the nation of the Jews afford as ſtrong a proof of their exiſtence as human nature is capable of giving and receiving upon any ſubject. For the wonders to which they had been eye-witneſſes, form the character of the nation, and which could not have been formed without real miracles. Whenever the characters of nations are different, we have no doubt that circumſtances did exiſt to form that character. There are many things done and ſaid in this country, that will always prove that we enjoyed a free conſtitution; even if a time ſhould come when no ſuch thing as a free conſtitution was to be found any where. And to my apprehenſion, the behaviour and opinions of the Jews prove as fully that they were directed by ſupernatural appearances; as the behaviour and opinions of the reſt of the world ſhew that they have formed themſelves upon natural appearances. For the character of the Jews is entirely diſtinct from the general ſuperſtitious character of mankind.

The weakneſs, knavery, credulity, and above all, the diſpoſition to lying, merely to gratify the delight

delight which moſt men take in hearing and re-
porting marvellous ſtories, ſeem to have perplexed
the opinions of mankind upon this ſubject. It
would not in the leaſt ſurprize me to hear a perſon affirm, that he himſelf has ſeen whatever has
been reported to have happened upon any occaſion. But the world knows how to make a proper
eſtimate of ſuch ſtories; and mankind in general
were never ſo weak as to be deceived by ſuch
things. For ſuch reports have univerſally loſt
their credit, ſometimes from the very beginning,
and always in a ſhort ſpace of time, either from
their want of importance, or their want of credibility; and are now only to be heard of becauſe
they furniſh an argument for infidels againſt the
miracles related in the Bible.

How comes it to paſs that theſe ſtories are ſo
univerſally acknowledged to be falſe, that they can
be ſafely uſed as inſtruments for undermining the
foundation of the goſpel miracles? The real
truth is this; where mankind were in earneſt,
they have always thought miracles too hazardous
a foundation to build upon; and accordingly no
impoſtors, who have had any important ſcheme in
hand, have ever meddled with miracles. Private
intercourſe with ſupernatural *beings* they have often
ventured to feign, becauſe in ſuch caſes they run
no hazard of detection, but the performing miracles openly in the face of the world, is what no
impoſtor ever attempted.

But if the things performed be not of the nature of thoſe which mankind are apt to forge, and
are not imitations of others, and are performed
openly before friend and foe, without any expectation raiſed beforehand, but only occaſionally;
and eſpecially if they make a part of a plan begun
long

long ago, and are attended with conſequences quite out of the reach of human foreſight, and alſo foreign to human purpoſes, theſe things are all to be taken into conſideration, and where all or moſt of theſe circumſtances concur, the moſt miraculous facts will ſupport their credit with every one who knows any thing of ſound reaſoning : and then even the very extraordinary nature of the facts will ſupport and confirm that very plan by which theſe ſupernatural events are in a certain ſenſe ſupported.

Every revelation muſt from the nature of the thing, and the faculties and circumſtances of men, be delivered with ſuch difficulties as would at firſt deſtroy its credibility, merely from the nature and ſingularity of the facts ; or if this be not ſo proper an expreſſion to convey my idea, it muſt put mankind upon inquiring after new grounds of conviction : for the opinions of mankind are founded in habits formed by the nature of things and by the whole courſe of our education, which will directly ſtand up againſt theſe ſupernatural facts, and will certainly overpower them unleſs ſome ſtrong motive rouſe the attention.

CHAP. X.

Of Chriſt's Kingdom.

BUT it has been matter of ſurprize, that miracles, which ought to have carried univerſal conviction along with them, being ſuited to the capacity of the moſt ignorant ſpectators, had no more effect upon the Jews, who were eye-witneſſes

neffes of them, than we find they had.   And this
makes it neceſſary to confider what were the circumſtances which ſo blinded the Jews as to prevent that conviction from being produced, which
was naturally to be expected ; and this ſeems prin-
cipally to have ariſen from the miſtakes of the Jews
concerning the nature of Chriſt's kingdom.   The
manner in which the Chriſtian diſpenſation is
ſpoken of in the prophetic language of the Old
Teſtament, joined to their own vanity, led the
Jews into a great miſtake concerning the nature of
this kingdom.   Such expreſſions as this, " and
" he ſhall reign over the houſe of Jacob for ever;
" and of his kingdom there ſhall be no end ;"
ſeem to foretel great temporal power and dominion.

   Our Saviour takes the greateſt pains to correct
their prejudices on this head, both by his conduct
and doctrine.   And in order to make his character
a conſiſtent one, and to agree with the predic-
tions concerning him, it was neceſſary that he
ſhould not raiſe the jealouſy of the Romans ; for
if he had been tried by them as a ſeditious perſon,
and condemned, he could not poſſibly have been
the Meſſiah of the prophets ; and how neceſſary
he himſelf thought it to keep up to this character,
appears evidently from his uſing the expreſſion ſo
often, that he did ſuch a thing that the Scriptures
might be fulfilled.   And the many prudential
ſteps which he is obſerved to take, have all the
ſame tendency : for he declares, that it is not from
any power or dread of his enemies, but only to
keep up to the character foretold of him, that he
takes ſuch ſteps as ſeem to imply ſome apprehenſions for himſelf.

Nor

Nor need we doubt but the Roman governor would have been alarmed if our Saviour had been followed by multitudes of tumultuous people: and accordingly we find his doctrines particularly calculated to diſcourage ſuch; and we may fairly conclude, that this, among other ends, was the intention of ſome of his longeſt addreſſes to the people. And the expreſſion which introduces the ſermon on the mount, is expreſs to this purpoſe: " And ſeeing the multitudes, &c." And it is very probable, that after the clear and poſitive manner in which he declares his ſentiments, as we find them delivered in this ſermon, theſe multitudes diſperſed very quietly, and with no ſmall diſappointment, upon finding that he was not the perſon they had taken him for.

Now, although from ſeeing his miracles they might be well ſatisfied that he had power to gratify all their wiſhes, yet, after ſuch an explicit declaration of his principles, they well knew that he never would comply with their inclinations. And the perverſe notions which the whole body of the Jews entertained upon this ſubject, give a particular force and propriety to the doctrines contained in the ſermon on the mount, when conſidered as intended to cure their prejudices concerning the nature of Chriſt's kingdom. And it was certainly a neceſſary part of his office, upon all occaſions, to ſet the Jews right in this particular, to ſhew them the impropriety of the Meſſiah's taking ſuch meaſures to eſtabliſh his kingdom, however great his power, which inſtead of reforming the manners of mankind, would give the Jews a licence for indulging themſelves in all kinds of exceſs, and would become a ſtanding

5 authority

authority for the practice of tyranny in all succeeding ages.

For if we confider the ftate of the Jews at the
time of our Saviour's coming, we may eafily imagine with what *fpirit* many of the people followed
him, upon feeing the miracles which he performed.
Efpecially as his miracles could leave them no
room to doubt, that he had certainly the power,
provided he had the inclination of reftoring the
kingdom to Ifrael. And the common principles
of human nature will tell us what would be their
expectations, when fuch an event took place. No
lefs, we may believe, than the expectation of
trampling their enemies under their feet; in
dulging themfelves in revenge for real or fuppofed
injuries; fhaking off the Roman yoke, and expecting befides an opportunity of gratifying every
fenfual appetite.

A people in fuch circumftances, and with fuch
expectations, ftood in need of conftant admonitions and informations to draw them out of their
error. And there muft have been a particular
air of authority in our Saviour's teaching, that
they could even bear to hear a doctrine carrying
fuch a particular fting with it, when confidered
as difappointing their fondeft hopes and expectations.

And that thefe reproofs and admonitions were
continued through the whole of our Saviour's
miniftry, may, among other reafons, be owing to
this, that the wifer fort of Jews might for fome
time imagine that he ufed policy to conceal his
real defigns, and only waited for a fit opportunity
to put them in execution; which was particularly
the cafe with his difciples: though it is alfo true

5   that

that the Jews, of the higher rank, were scandalized at the mean character which he assumed.

But at length the whole nation, putting all circumstances together, gave up all hopes of deliverance through his means; having been frequently disappointed both by his miracles and doctrine: the former confirming them more and more in their notions of his irresistible power, and the little occasion which he had for watching favourable opportunities to put any scheme in execution; while the latter would convince them that they could expect no benefit from him in the only way which they wished.

And thus the joint influence of his doctrine and miracles produced a most extraordinary, though a very natural effect among the Jews, and what neither of them could have done singly. For their minds, having been so long agitated between hope and fear, they felt their disappointment so sensibly, that it was followed by the hatred and detestation of the whole people, which shewed itself with aggravated maliciousness, unparalleled in the history of any nation. For their behaviour when he was condemned, and at the time of his crucifixion, shews the spiteful gratification which they enjoyed in thinking that they had been able to destroy a power which they could not turn to their own advantage.

And thus the very worst part of the behaviour of the Jews is a strong proof that they had seen and believed the miracles of our Saviour; and the reality of the miracles is one of the causes why the Jews reject Christ for their Saviour. Even Barabbas, or any sower of sedition, would answer the expectations of such a people better, than the mild and upright Jesus, with the power of working miracles.

N C H A P.

CHAP. XI.

Of the Propagation of the Gospel.

WE are told by St. Mark, that before our Saviour left the world, he gave this commiſſion
to his diſciples; " And he ſaid unto them, Go ye
" into all the world, and preach the goſpel to
" every creature." This is certainly a very extraordinary commiſſion, in whatever point of view
it is conſidered. For an undertaking of this ſort
has numberleſs difficulties attending it, from the
extenſive nature of the plan, even if the execution were to be attended with every favourable
circumſtance; ſuch as a people naturally diſpoſed
to learn, and teachers properly qualified to execute
the orders which they had received. What opinion would a thinking man be apt to entertain
of the ſucceſs of ſuch a ſcheme, upon taking into
the account the obſtinacy and unteachable diſpoſition of mankind, joined to a natural averſion
from the principles which it was propoſed to communicate to them? Surely he would be apt to
conclude from the perverſe nature of man, and
his proneneſs to evil, that this taſk, though it was
nothing but laying goodneſs and virtue before all
mankind, could never be enjoined by one " who
" knew what was in man," but ought rather to be
looked upon, as the benevolent effuſion of a heart
conſcious of its own uprightneſs, but without the
leaſt experience of human affairs.

But when the character and learning of thoſe
to whom this commiſſion is delivered are taken
into

into confideration, every one would be ready to declare, that this was certainly a very harmlefs commiffion, but the moft ridiculous that ever was given, and a thing that, in the event, muft ruin the character of its author, if he had any to lofe.

We find Livy producing the following argument as conclufive againft the common opinion, that Numa received his inftruction from Pythagoras; " Ex quibus locis, etfi ejufdem ætatis fuiflet, " qua fama in Sabinos aut quo linguæ commercio " quenquam ad cupiditatem difcendi excivifſet ; " quove præfidio, unus per tot gentes, diflonas " fermone moribufque perveniffet ? "

With what propriety might thefe queftions have been afked upon the occafion of this miffion of eleven fifhermen, from fo fmall a corner of the globe as Judea, and even from the moft contemptible part of that little fpot, which had been induftrioufly feparated from the reft of the world, both in religion and language.

Well might it have been afked, What reputation had thefe fifhermen acquired, either for learning, or the arts of perfuafion, (for they could not fpeak their own language with propriety) that they, of all others, fhould be employed, with the leaft probable expectation, that even their own countrymen would liften to their doctrine, had it been in no wife inconfiftent with their prejudices.

Yet what are we to think when their commiffion extended not only to the inftructing of their own countrymen, nor indeed fimply to the teaching of all mankind, but to no lefs an object than the reformation of the whole world ; not from ordinary ignorance and corruption, but from thofe corrup-

tions

tions and errors which have the deepest root in human nature, as springing directly from those paſſions and enjoyments which mankind are moſt greedily addicted to.

Surely it might very naturally be made a queſtion, By what intercourſe of language, were they to deliver their ſentiments in ſuch a manner as to be able to raiſe the expectations, and fix the attention of thoſe to whoſe language they were perfect ſtrangers, and whoſe morals, religion, and ſettled cuſtoms they were to aboliſh or reform ?

Or, Who was to guard them in their journey through ſo many nations, differing not only from them, but alſo from one another, in their language and manners ?

If we had nothing but report, that ſuch a ſcheme had been ſet on foot, and that it had ſucceeded, notwithſtanding all theſe unfavourable circumſtances ; and if any ſtreſs ſhould be laid on ſuch a ſtory, as an argument for bridling the paſſions of mankind, how loud would our preſent race of freethinkers be in their declamations, and how poſitive in their reaſonings, that human nature was by no means able to ſupport the credit of ſuch a ſtory ; and that the very mention of ſuch a thing as the work of man, carried a direct and poſitive lie along with it ; or, to uſe the expreſſion of a free-thinker, that the argument againſt it was as ſtrong as any argument from experience could be.

But now that the fact is evident and certain, and even ſenſible to our daily experience ; all this turns out to be the craft and cunning of thoſe ſimple and illiterate fiſhermen ; working upon the minds of ſimple people violently addicted to their

own

own prejudices, whoſe language and manners they were ſtrangers to.

Now, although this opinion of the free-thinkers can never be taken up by any rational creature, who is in the leaſt acquainted with the circumſtances of this hiſtory; yet the paſſions and inclinations of mankind, and the whole courſe of worldly affairs, are ſuch enemies to the truths which the goſpel conveys, that the thoughts of men may be eaſily turned away from paying a proper attention to ſuch ſubjects; by the little plauſible cávils of infidels, did not Chriſtian ſocieties keep up a ſucceſſion of men to watch over the intereſts of religion, and refute ſuch objections as might daily ariſe.

And this ſeems to me to be moſt effectually done, by pointing out the extenſive plan of religion, and particularly by explaining and inſiſting upon thoſe points which diſtinguiſh this ſcheme from natural events and human projects, and particularly by fixing our attention upon thoſe grand events, when God ſeems compleatly to have taken this work out of the hands of men.

Now, the manner in which the Chriſtian Religion has been propagated, is undoubtedly one of the ſtrongeſt arguments for its divine original; and the wonderful gift of tongues is certainly one of the chief inſtruments of its propagation: it may therefore be proper, in this argument, to inquire a little particularly into the nature, dignity, and influence of this extraordinary gift, as a proof that this religion comes from God, by ſhewing that it never could have ſuited human purpoſes to feign pretenſions to ſuch a gift; and that it is only in the hand of God that its uſe and importance can be ſeen.

N 3 It

It is reafonable to conclude, from the behaviour of the difciples, at the time when our Saviour delivered their commiffion to them, that this extraordinary injunction of teaching all the world, did not appear to them to be by any means above their power to perform: they make no remonftrances, as we find Mofes doing upon a much lefs affair, and in very different circumftances. For although they had no conception of the manner or means by which this great work was to be brought about, yet inftead of fhewing any backwardnefs to undertake it, we have good reafon to think, that they were difpofed to fet about its execution without the proper qualification; otherwife it could not have been neceffary to give it them in charge not to depart from Jerufalem, but *wait for the promife of the Father.*

This confidence is not difficult to be accounted for, becaufe it feems naturally to have arifen from the frequent fupernatural exertions of power to which they had been accuftomed, or rather habituated; and which they could have no doubt would be fufficient for any purpofe; and as they had experienced already in themfelves the power of working miracles, they might conceive this power to be adequate to all their purpofes; and fo we may believe the generality of mankind would have thought. And although their Mafter had told them that the fpeaking with tongues was to be one of the figns of thofe who were to believe, yet I am well perfuaded that they were not then fully fenfible of the great advantage of this gift; much lefs of the neceffity of it for the purpofe of their miffion.

But God, who knows the nature of man, knew alfo that the fulleft power of working miracles or wonders,

wonders, would not be ſufficient for this grand purpoſe of deſtroying the kingdom of Satan, and reforming the world.

If, indeed, there had been nothing farther pro-poſed, than to raiſe the wonder and admiration of the nations, (which would have been the only end which an impoſtor could propoſe to himſelf) and to play upon their credulity, and to turn their fears and ſimplicity to worldly advantage, the working of wonders would have been the deſirable gift. And this gift of tongues would have ap-peared ſo inadequate to the ſchemes and views of an impoſtor; that the feigning of it never could have been ſuggeſted to him by his wants, upon any occaſion, as his deſign is only to deceive, and not to reform, and therefore could hardly be ſup-poſed to enter into his head; or if it had, the advantage of it would have appeared ſo trifling, that he never could have entertained a wiſh for a qualification, of which he could neither conceive the uſe nor importance.

This, however, will be ſtill more evident, if we take a curſory view of the ends propoſed by the different pretenders to ſupernatural power, or the particular favour and aſſiſtance of the gods. The plan of ſuch impoſtors is not to teach man-kind; to what purpoſe then would it be to pre-tend to a gift, which could be only of uſe where ſomething was to be communicated to the people of a ſtrange language? Eſpecially when we con-ſider ſuch pretenſions as coming from one who could have no other ſcheme than what was, in ſome way or other, to anſwer his own temporal purpoſes; which would certainly be brought about moſt effectually by exciting terror, wonder, or admiration. And ſurely to hear a ſtranger ſpeaking

in

in one's own tongue, is not the likelieſt means of raiſing theſe paſſions.

The fruits of an impoſtor's labours muſt be near in proſpect; whatever was to look very far into futurity, could have no charms for him, but more particularly with ſo diſmal a proſpect as the Chriſtian Religion exhibited at its firſt ſetting out in the world. For this religion, even after our Saviour's aſcenſion, had a great deal leſs than nothing to engage the attention of a deceiver, ſuppoſing his ambition to have been of that moderate kind which is to be gratified by the diſtant view of propagating an opinion once to become general, for even this ſmall gratification had every human probability againſt it.

But let us conſider thoſe uſes to which mankind have applied their pretenſions to ſupernatural power or aid; and by examining theſe, it will be eaſy to conjecture of what account ſuch pretenders would have held the gift of tongues.

Princes and rulers made uſe of ſuch pretenſions, to eaſe themſelves of the very great trouble of governing a paſſionate, ignorant, and diſorderly multitude; or, to ſpeak more properly, perhaps ſuch pretenſions were neceſſary to render ſuch a government by any means practicable; becauſe the paſſions of a lawleſs, ignorant multitude, could never be kept within any bounds by pretenſions merely human; ignorance not being capable of liſtening to reaſon, but only of being affected by ſuch things as raiſe wonder and dread. Peace, therefore, would be the object of ſuch pretenders to ſupernatural power; and terrible things, ſuch as alarm the minds of men, would be the inſtruments neceſſary for this purpoſe, and ſuch as princes and rulers would wiſh for the poſſeſſion of: and what they had not in their power, their whole art and induſtry would be employed in feigning, as far as they could hope for credit, ſuch pretenſiohs being abſolutely neceſſary for their purpoſe: and liars by profeſſion would make an eſſential part of ſuch a government, not the enthuſiaſtic liar, but the ſober, ſedate impoſtor.

When his ſubjects became clamorous or unruly, a prince would never think that the faculty of ſpeaking to them in an unknown tongue was what his government, upon that emergency, required: all his wiſhes and ambition would be to have the darting of Jupiter's thunder; and all his lying and impoſition would tend to propagate an opinion among mankind, either that he was poſſeſſed of it, or if that could not be, at leaſt that he could command it; as there were certain actions that would infallibly bring it down. And by ſuch lying wonders was the kingdom of Satan eſtabliſhed in the world.

There have alſo been in the world an inferior kind of pretenders to ſupernatural power, known by the name of ſorcerers, whoſe ſole end was to delude the vulgar, and ſuch as have vulgar underſtandings, out of a little money, in exchange for their art; whoſe influence could never extend beyond the procuring a precarious ſubſiſtence from the credulity and admiration of the multitude.

Dread and terror, therefore, would be the paſſions which princes and rulers would endeavour chiefly to inſpire into their ſubjects; and the whole force of the ſorcerer's art would be employed in raiſing the wonder and admiration of the multitude; and thus it would become the aim and intereſt of both theſe kinds of pretenders, that

many

many stories should be propagated to raise and keep up these several passions; which would all contain much of the marvelous to gratify the natural desires of the people, who in their rude state are only to be pleased with such narrations; and these stories would, in some measure, form the characters of their gods, who indeed are easily traced to the mould in which they were cast. Nothing, therefore, could have been so useless, or so hazardous, as the pretension to a gift of tongues, for all the purposes which impostors and pretenders to supernatural aid or power have had to answer by their forgeries.

Let us next consider how well it suits with the Christian scheme, and how essentially necessary it was for carrying on God's plan in the world. This, indeed, is very different from the views either of kings or sorcerers, being such as are by no means suited to mere human wants or human prospects. By this scheme mankind were neither to be terrified, surprized, or amused, but they were to be taught and reformed; nor was this object the reformation or instruction of a few individuals; but the command is to teach all mankind; " go ye into all the world, and preach the gospel " to every creature."

But how is this task to be performed? Even the working of miracles would be, by no means, sufficient for this purpose; for it could answer no good end to alarm the fears, and rouse the attention of mankind, if nothing was to follow: for their attention would be gained to no purpose, if no instruction or reformation was to follow or accompany such marvellous works; the teacher would nevertheless be a barbarian among those whose language he was ignorant of. The gift of

tongues

tongues, therefore, was abſolutely neceſſary for the propagation of the goſpel in that full manner which was intended and accompliſhed.

The Supreme Being ſeems but little careful to ſuit his diſpenſations to thoſe forms which moſt readily draw the attention, and gain the admiration or approbation of men; and therefore it is that the wiſe men of this world are not taken with the moſt ſignal marks of God's interpoſition, as they are paſſing before their eyes; but nevertheleſs they ſeem to be admirably calculated for engaging the wonder and admiration of the ſerious and thinking part of mankind, particularly of poſterity, when they are properly diſpoſed to take a ſerious view of the ſubject: and eſpecially we of this age have much greater opportunities, and are better qualified to judge of the greatneſs and good effects of this miracle of the gift of tongues, than if we had lived at the very time when it happened; and, I may add, than if we had heard the Apoſtles ſpeak with thoſe very tongues. For we can trace the good effects of it through many regions of the earth, and thus form a proper notion of its uſe and importance, and alſo come to be fully perſuaded that this commiſſion of teaching all nations was the moſt important, the moſt neceſſary, and the hardeſt to be put in practice of all others.

For although it was a neceſſary, it was not an eaſy leſſon which the nations were to be taught; it was not a bare ignorance which was to be overcome, but rooted and inveterate prejudices which were to be got the better of: in ſhort, the kingdom of Satan was to be aboliſhed, which had got ſuch a firm footing in the hearts of men, that no human power was a match for it. Indeed,

as

as to human arts, the kingdom of Satan was already in poffeffion of them ; and *the rulers of the darkneſs of this world,* had applied every one of them to their own purpofes, in fome fhape or other : and becaufe particularly at the time of our Saviour's coming, if we take an impartial view of the ftate of the heathens, this kingdom feems to have been the moft firmly eftablifhed, having, befides the arts, got all the moft violent human paffions and defires on its fide.

Now it can hardly be doubted that proper meditations upon fuch a victory as this ought to operate more effectually upon a well-informed and well-difpofed mind, than any tranfient acts of power exhibited to the fenfes, however great they might be.

And thus, this fingle gift of tongues, confidered in its caufes and its confequences, appears of itfelf to be a conclufive argument for 'the truth of the Chriftian Religion, ferving admirably to diftinguifh the immediate works of God from the forgeries and pretended wonders of impoftors of all kinds. And this argument I confider as conclufive ; becaufe, if the finger of God is to be feen for certain in any part of this work of the propagation of the gofpel, I do not confider the proof as in the leaft affected by objections brought againft particular parts of this fcheme : not even if it fhould be fhewn that human arts had no fmall fhare in the propagation of Chriftianity, and other means which have little appearance of a divine original.

The truth or falfhood of fuch affertions, I am not concerned with at prefent, becaufe I contend that if they were even true, my argument is not in the leaft affected by them, as they may be conceived

ceived as parts of a plan very conſiſtent with God's method of governing the world. For it is not ſo much the things that are ſaid, as the manner of ſaying them, that can give any juſt grounds to conclude that ſuch objections are made with any view or intention unfriendly to religion.

But there is a very unphiloſophical way which the free-thinkers have got into of ſuppoſing particular attributes to belong to God, not like the faculties of a free agent, but rather as moulded into the form and nature of definitions, from which notions every thing relating to the Deity is to be derived conſequentially ; like mathematical concluſions from the properties of extenſion. And thus they ſet about trying the circumſtances of a revelation by theſe notions of their own : and very impiouſly pretend to ſay, that particular things or plans are unworthy of God, without paying any attention to matter of fact. Now this is not ſimply bad divinity, but it is according to the plan of the very worſt philoſophy that ever appeared in the world. But if ſuch reaſoners, laying aſide their own imaginations, would attend to facts as delivered in Scripture, they will find a conſiſtent plan carrying on through the whole : and that this plan is not ſo much carried on according to the glorious attributes which we very juſtly aſcribe to God, as according to that weakneſs which we find in man. In diſpenſing the bleſſings of a revelation, the Supreme Being does not ſo much appear in his majeſty, as in the more humble character of a teacher of the human race ; neither overpowering their underſtandings, nor forcing their wills. It is only " he that " hath ears to hear, let him hear ;" leaving men free agents, and yet throwing circumſtances in
their

their way, which, by a proper ufe of their fenfes and underftandings, will certainly lead them to happinefs, and bring human nature to as great a degree of perfection as it is capable to be brought, making every thing as much as poffible feem to be the work of men. And therefore this very fcheme, to a fuperficial obferver, might feem to partake of human weaknefs, when it is, in fact, the greateft proof of condefcenfion and wifdom.

And befides, the providence of God appears to permit that men fhould mix in this plan, what may be properly called their own, when it will anfwer the purpofe; and thefe parts the infidel fixes upon, and contends that all the reft is to be referred to the fame original.

But furely it is no difficult thing to conceive, that it may be very eafy for fuch a *Being* as the Deift himfelf allows God to be, to make a perfect creature: therefore he might, no doubt, at once have given human nature all the perfection of which it is capable. Yet furely it is a much greater difplay of wifdom to contrive matters fo as to make fuch a being as man, with all his imperfections about him, fo very inftrumental in perfecting his own nature, as he is made to be according to the plan which I have been endeavouring to explain.

Eleven fifhermen fet out from Judæa, without learning, and even without any proper notions of the bufinefs they were about, as appears from the very laft queftion that they afk our Saviour, " Lord, wilt thou, at this time, reftore the king-" dom to Ifrael?" They fet out to inftruct the world in a new religion, and, what was more difficult, to deftroy the old, which had the fupport of power, prejudices, paffion, and intereft, being modelled

modelled according to the wiſhes of mankind. Nobody ſurely but God, could give the leaſt proſpect of ſucceſs to ſuch an unreaſonable undertaking.

How different were the ſchemes of philoſophers for improving mankind, ſo very excellent in themſelves, that they will never perhaps appear mean, upon any occaſion, except upon a compariſon with this teaching. A philoſopher thought it practicable to communicate a few notions, which were at variance with no particular paſſions or appetites; and this he had hopes of doing with ſucceſs, to a few only of thoſe who ſpoke the ſame language, and who had alſo the ſame manners and diſpoſitions.

But what would he have thought of the propoſal of teaching the whole world; all nations, however different their language, and however various their manners and humours? And to teach them, not ſuch things as are ſuitable, and even agreeable to human frailty, or might flatter human pride; but ſuch things as every one to whom they were propoſed, would be ready to ſay, " theſe are hard " ſayings; who can hear them? "

In ſhort, this is ſuch a plan as hath nothing in common with the learning of philoſophers, or the ſchemes of politicians, or the tricks of impoſtors; nor indeed hath it any thing in it of the nature of man: and yet, what is very ſurprizing, ſo much hath God accommodated himſelf to the nature of man, in the ſeveral human inſtruments that he has made uſe of, that an argument has been formed ſufficient to miſlead thoſe, who take only a partial view of things, into an opinion as if the whole was a work of human contrivance. Now this diſpenſation, on the contrary, appears to have a wonderful

wonderful beauty in it, at the fame time that it difplays the wifdom of God, by fetting that wifdom in a point of view, in which it could not have appeared without fuch a frail creature as man to work with. For by permitting men to mix of their own, provided it was true, and to the purpofe, with whatever he communicates to them, God has beautifully adapted this fcheme to the human capacity, by making as much of it as poffible the work of man.

So that whatever human interpofition can be fhewn to have taken place in the propagation of the gofpel, appears to be a beauty in this fyftem, and is what one might expect from the general plan of God's providence: the main argument not being in the leaft affected by this conceffion, fo long as the entire fcheme is beyond the power of human contrivance, and even after it was contrived beyond the power of man to execute.

C H A P. XII.

Of the Perfection of the Chriftian Religion.

THE Chriftian Religion, if once believed to be true, affords the compleateft fatisfaction to the mind; and leaves us nothing beyond either to hope or fear: for it fully fatisfies the paffions both of hope and fear, which are by no means the eafieft to gratify of thofe found in human nature.

To fay nothing of the heathen fuperftitions, even the Jewifh difpenfation is very imperfect, and can afford no real fatisfaction to the mind: it is
only

only a fcheme in *embryo*, though fupported and carried on by divine affiftance and authority, and is by no means capable of fatisfying the mind with regard to any of thofe material points upon which we want information moft. It does not bring life and immortality to light. It exhibits God as partial, condefcending to become the teacher and conductor of a particular people, very fmall in comparifon of the bulk of mankind, at the fame time that he leaves the reft cf the world to follow their own inventions.

But the Chriftian fcheme is compleat from the time that our Saviour faid, " It is finifhed;" there was nothing farther neceffary but to publifh to the world what had been done ; and this was particularly the office of the Holy Spirit to do. We have no farther information to expect on this fubject, nor is it probable that human nature is capable of receiving any more ; what remains being fuch things " as eyes have not feen, nor ears heard, " neither hath it entered into the heart of man to " conceive."

The great plan for the redemption of mankind is finifhed in this world whenever this religion is univerfally underftood and acknowledged ; when mankind are made fenfible of the nature and caufe of their infirmities, and the proper remedies for them : and then human nature will be fo far corrected and reformed, and all irregular paffions fubdued, fo far at leaft that we may begin another world with much greater advantages, than we fhould have done this, even if Adam had not fallen : fo that the whole will doubtlefs appear a beautiful and wife and good and confiftent plan ; and the evils which we fee, or pretend to fee, will be found to be imaginary, or perhaps real good,

O

or

or elfe will be rectified or done away. What an
infight into human nature will the day of judgement alone give, when the fecrets of all hearts
will be laid open! What a leffon will this be for
our future behaviour in the ftate where we may
be placed. This world will then appear to advantage, as a ftate of probation, and we fhall be able
to proceed with confidence, by feeing experimentally what human nature, affifted by the Chriftian
Religion, can do, or has been able to do; and by
having a perfect fenfe of the ill behaviour of ourfelves and others, this will be fufficient warning
againft becoming the flaves of temptations however artfully engaging.

No man that believes fincerely in the Chriftian
Religion, can want any farther information; he
knows his beginning, and is alfo fufficiently informed of his end: he fees that God has interefted
himfelf too much in the affairs of this world, not
to be fully perfuaded that he will finifh con-
fiftently what he has conducted fo far. And from
the wonderful difplay of power which has been
made in this world, we may be perfuaded that a
fituation will be prepared for us, of which at prefent we can form no conception, it being far beyond the reach of human imagination, and effentially different from thofe notions which the heathens had of a future ftate, which obvioufly be-
tray their original, by the refemblance which they
bear to the little partial prejudices of mankind.
But there is one extraordinary weaknefs that fticks
to their fcheme, which is this, that though they
ftrip mankind of their bodies in a future ftate, yet
they were obliged to confine their happinefs to
fenfual pleafures, or at leaft fuch as were enjoyed
by them in this world; and thefe, for want of

3   organs,

organs, they are reduced to the neceſſity of abridging very much, ſo that a heathen future ſtate is nothing even to this world for enjoyment.

But mark, on the other hand, the difference between this and the rewards propoſed by the Chriſtian Religion: though the grand doctrine of this religion is the reſurrection of the body, yet we are carried to gratifications entirely ſpiritual, and ſuch as we, while inhabitants of this world, can have no conception of. No reſemblance to any thing in this world, is promiſed us in the next, it will be ſomething entirely new: and thus only could it be worthy of the mighty *apparatus* which has been made for it.

We may know from our own experience, that none of the fabulous accounts of the elyſian fields could afford us the leaſt ſatisfaction, and that every rational man muſt turn from them with contempt, even if he believed them to be true; and with very unfavourable notions of the attributes of the gods, for not being able to provide for mankind a future ſtate equal in enjoyment to this world.

And this ought to give great ſatisfaction to a Chriſtian, and even ſtrengthen his faith, that he has ſomething to expect which muſt far ſurpaſs any thing which his own imagination can reach. And thus God's ways will be found wonderfully wiſe, both with regard to what he diſcovers to us, and in what he conceals, thus raiſing our expectations upon good grounds, from earthly to heavenly things, and from material and corporeal to ſpiritual enjoyments. And even this diſpenſation, if ſeriouſly conſidered, will make a very ſtrong argument for the truth of our religion, by diſcovering that the whole plan is wonderfully of a piece.

No

No fteps taken to pre-engage the attention of mankind, no flattering them with gaudy profpects, or with the gratification of fuch paffions as engage our chief attention in this world. The whole fyftem keeps one uniform tenor, every thing is fet fairly before man, and he may attend to, or neglect this information at his peril.

The neceffities and circumftances of men urge them on to a fpeedy execution of their projects, and make them force prematurely into light every thing that can engage the attention of the world. And this is their wifdom, being only children of a day, and even ignorant what that day may bring forth. But the Supreme Being, who has all eternity at his command, can execute his plans in whatever manner he pleafes, and is not likely to condefcend to humour the unreafonable with that kind of evidence which they fancy fhould be laid before them, which is very *modeftly* requiring that God fhould work after their plan : but he goes on to act according to his own, which we are required to attend to, and expect nothing elfe.

And the human agents whom God has employed in this work of our redemption, difcover the original from whence they derive their knowledge, by their manner of acting. The important office with which they are entrufted, never raifes their pride fo as to make them forget that they have this gift in earthen veffels, and therefore they dif-cover no impatience, but wait for their information with all due humility. But this is never the way by which impoftors proceed ; they fhew not only a willingnefs, but even a forwardnefs to gratify thofe whofe attention they would engage ; and by profeffing and promifing too much, difcover that they can do nothing.

Human

Human nature may, in this world, exhibit all the different temptations to which flesh and blood can be liable, and they may all have been re-fisted by different men, though that degree of per-fection is not to be expected from any single indi-vidual; and this may be a kind of practical stan-dard of what human nature can do, or at least pre-pare us for the reception of those favours which our Saviour will certainly bestow upon those who sincerely believe in him.

And thus men may be prepared by the discipline of this world, so as to be fit for the future state in which they are to be placed, with a power over their passions acquired by experience. And they may be made capable of the greatest enjoyment, without any danger of running into excess, and abusing the favours of Christ; having their facul-ties so suited to the means of gratification, that they may be safely allowed the prospect of all sorts of enjoyments, and objects of temptation, without the danger of committing such a sin as the eating the forbidden fruit.

O 3 T H E

THE

CONCLUSION.

I Have now finifhed my argument, in which the very difficulties which we find in Revelation, are confidered as one very ftrong proof of its divine authority. My principles do not lead to any dogmatical conclufions, but rather to engage the mind, at an awful diftance, to take a profpect of the natural world, of mankind, and of religion. They are all the work of God, and may all three be ftudied to the great improvement of human nature.

The facts, upon which the evidence for the Chriftian Religion refts, are fo fingular, fo ftriking, fo numerous, and connected together for fuch a length of time, that there feems nothing to prevent the opinions of mankind from being more uniform upon this fubject, than upon any other whatever. The candidates for the kingdom of heaven have no occafion for harbouring any of thofe jealoufies that perplex and inflame the little factious contefts of worldly-minded men.

However, when we confider that the world has been fo often deluded by falfe pretences to infpiration, and fupernatural affiftance, it is both neceffary, and for the credit of our religion, that the grounds of our belief fhould undergo a very ferious and impartial examination. And although

I have

I have endeavoured to ſhew that human reaſon is very unequal to the taſk, either of diſcovering or propagating a true religion, yet it is the beſt natural means which we have of ſecuring ourſelves from being impoſed upon by a falſe one. And we are even commanded in Scripture to " be " ready to give an anſwer to every one who aſks " us a reaſon of the hope which is in us."

Nor has the preſent age been backward in furniſhing us with occaſion for practiſing this part of our duty. For we have been harraſſed by infidel writers with objections phyſical, metaphyſical, and philological; and in the characters of Jews, Turks, and Buffoons.

It is not the objections made to the Chriſtian Religion that I find fault with, it is the manner in which they are made and received. One might at leaſt expect that a pure religion, calculated to ſupply every defect which the mind finds in itſelf, would at leaſt be as favourably received as an ordinary piece of good news, and would only leave the mind in a ſtate of anxiety and ſuſpence, but with our ears open to every argument which could ſtrengthen our conviction, from an apprehenſion that it might not be true. But many write, and are heard againſt Chriſtianity, with ſuch a ſpirit and diſpoſition, as could only be juſtifiable if the whole ſcheme and intention of it was to bring deſtruction to the human race.

A ſecond thing deſerving blame in the conduct of infidel writers, is their diſcharging their arrows at random, without any ſettled ſcheme but that of doing miſchief. The moſt plauſible pretence for infidelity being the dangerous and pernicious conſequences of ſuperſtition, if the free-thinkers were true to this principle, they ought to join with

us

us in eftablifhing Chriftianity, as we have the proof of experience, as I have fhewn in this argument, that it is the only fure bulwark againft fuperftition.

For the abfurd notions which even the wifeft men of antiquity entertained upon religious fubjects, prove beyond all difpute, that no degree of mere human wifdom is a fufficient guard for us againft becoming the dupes of the groffeft fuperftitions. They, therefore, who are for bringing down religion to the teft and ftandard of human reafon, would do well to confider, that if they were to fucceed in their fcheme, and deftroy the credit of the Chriftian Religion, mankind would naturally fall back into their original fuperftitions, and become the dupes of their own fears and of frefh impoftors.

The infidels, therefore, if they underftood their own fcheme, (which makes me fufpect that they have no other befides that of bringing a railing accufation againft religion) ought to confefs that a belief in the Chriftian Religion, is the greateft advance that ever has been made towards perfecting their plan; and therefore they ought to take breath and look around them, and confider whether this is not as much as human nature can bear in the way of a reformation from fuperftition. Becaufe, without proper notions of God, and a well authenticated account of his manner of dealing with mankind, we fhall always be flaves to endlefs fuperftitions. We contend, that the Bible contains all this in the greateft perfection; the infidels fhould either produce a more authentic account than ours, or if they find that impoffible, try to overlook or mend the flaws which they pretend to difcover in ours, as this is the beft

remedy

remedy which the nature of things can bear. Pulling to pieces and demoliſhing, is a good mob-amuſement, but a time will come when every one muſt ſeek for ſhelter: and therefore it would be but rational and proper to look forward, and take a view of the habitation which is preparing for us by theſe projectors.

But neither this world, nor the next, can ſubſiſt upon the infidel plan: for if we were to allow that a ſolitary Atheiſt might exiſt, a nation of Atheiſts is as great a contradiction to uniform experience, as any abſurdity which can be imagined: and it would be juſt as wiſe a project to ſet about twiſting ropes of ſand, as to try to unite Atheiſts in a ſociety. An Atheiſt may cling to a ſociety, as ſome creeping weeds do to trees, and while he is corrupting it, may be conſidered by fools as an ornament to it. Freethinkers and ſubtle thinkers are the froth of ſociety, which is only kept at the top by the fermentation of the *ſub-ſtance* below.

Mankind will, therefore, always have gods of ſome kind or another, and conſequently a religion; and it lies upon the infidels to prove that it will be ſuch a rational one as Chriſtianity. We find that every ſpecies of knowledge has its proper organ of conveyance to the mind: ſounds come in by the ear, and colours by the eye, but to judge of Religion as ſome men do, ſeems to be acting as wiſely, as if one were to judge of the ſmooth-neſs of a ſurface by his ſmell.

We ſhould be told particularly what the diſco-veries are which would compleatly overturn the Chriſtian Religion, and then one could form ſome eſtimate how near the infidels are to the compleat-ing of their taſk. Becauſe in an affair of ſuch

6

general

general importance as religion, it is abfolutely neceffary that every man fhould have fome fettled
opinion; and it therefore becomes his duty, after
the moft diligent fearch, to fit down contented
with the beft opinion which he has been able to
form, and to reft fatisfied with that evidence which
the nature of the fubject will admit of, without
trifling with himfelf, or fuffering himfelf to be
trifled with by others: but efpecially before he determines againft the Chriftian Religion, it may be
ufeful for him to confider, that whenever things
admit of demonftrative proof, it can be proved
with equal clearnefs, that one thing is falfe, and
another true; therefore, if one determine to reft
fatisfied with nothing lefs than demonftration, why
fall in with the opinions of infidels? How do
they prove that there is no God? How do they
prove that he does not conduct the affairs of this
world? They ought not to be fatisfied with making objections to our fcheme of revelation; let
them take the pofitive fide, and eftablifh a fyftem
of infidelity, without fuppofing that there ever
was fuch a thing as religion in the world; I mean,
to write a fyftem of faith for mankind, without
taking any notice of revelation. Nothing could
more effectually fhew the poverty of infidelity, than
an attempt at a work of this kind, which would
be found to confift of negatives without a fingle
pofitive fact to reft upon: and it is at leaft as great
a reflexion upon infidelity to be fupported by weak
arguments, as it would be for religion to be defended by fuch. God we fay has delivered this
religion to the world, we do not pretend to be the
authors of it, nor even to comprehend it; and
therefore are neither obliged, nor capable to explain it fully: if it was our own work, we might
be

be reasonably asked to account for every thing in it. Now the system of infidels is their own work, and therefore they ought to be able to give a full and rational account of it, and fix the opinions of their disciples upon something positive, and not content themselves with denying things to be facts which we alledge are so; they must have a poor claim to be facts indeed, if they would not be ill exchanged for the dreams of infidelity. And un- · til the infidels can produce stronger arguments in proof of their principles, even if nothing were al- ledged against them, it is not so clear a point that religion is an imposition upon mankind, as that a prudent man would depend upon it.

. And indeed I would require no more of a man when he examines the arguments for and against revelation, than to carry his worldly prudence along with him, and to act with the same caution in his spiritual concerns, as he does in his tempo- ral affairs, about which, I am sorry to say it, man- kind are more sincere and in earnest than about religion.

But if the view of the Christian Religion, which I have taken, be a true one, it carries a very alarming appearance with regard to such unbe- lievers, and a very serious appearance with regard to the whole human race. The scheme seems fairly and fully laid before mankind, and they may attend to it or neglect it as they please, with- out any further information or warning. No dis- position is shewn to humour conceited men with occasional satisfaction. This religion keeps on its course with a solemn and awful steadiness, as far above all partiality. And having accompanied human nature, and seen all its powers and weak- nesses, its perfections and imperfections, the

Christian

Chriftian Religion is then with awful majefty to fhut up the fcene of mortality.

The fporting of an infidel with fuch a plan as this, is a ferious madnefs: and the ferious attempt to fetter it in human fyftems, would be but badly reprefented by the folly of him who fhould think of ftopping the waves of the ocean with a grain of fand.

Let us therefore examine with care and awful attention the progrefs of fuch a religion, which both promifes and threatens fo much; nor fuffer ourfelves to be laughed out of our hopes of immortality by the unfeafonable buffoonery of wits and libertines, nor try to reft that faith upon human fyftems, nor upon any fuch principles, which ftands upon FACTS, and ought to ftand upon no other foundation than that of the apoftles and prophets, Jefus Chrift himfelf being the chief corner ftone.

Another thing very proper to be attended to by every ferious inquirer after religious truth, is this; that the condition in which we are here placed, naturally fuppofes that we fhould not have the cleareft evidence for things belonging to revelation: but rather fuch as would have a tendency to keep the mind in a ftate of fufpence. For as the providence of God is carrying on two fchemes at the fame time, by the fame agents, it is impoffible for us to fay how far a clear difcovery of the one might be confiftent with the other.

We find that fometimes even imaginary views of a future ftate are fufficiently engaging to deftroy all relifh for the enjoyments of the prefent: how much more, then, might we expect the fame confequence from a clear view of the reality? the joys of which the Scripture confirms to be fo

great

great, that it hath not entered into the heart of man to conceive them.

Beſides, the very nature of a ſtate of probation, in the ſenſe in which it has been explained in this argument, ſeems to imply an evidence encumbered with many difficulties, both from the part that mankind are allowed to take in carrying on this ſcheme, and alſo from the various inſtruments made uſe of in carrying it on. And where would be the merit in reſiſting a temptation to gratify an ordinary appetite, in order to obtain a great and durable good, unleſs the proſpect of it was both remote, and attended with ſome uncertainty.

We may, therefore, reſt aſſured, that God in his infinite wiſdom intended his revelation ſhould be incumbered with, and involved in all its preſent difficulties, as a trial of our faith, an exerciſe of our patience, and a proof of our teachable diſpoſition ; and that even thus it is better fitted for anſwering our purpoſes, than if it had leſs of the myſterious in it.

Laſtly, when we are engaged in a ſubject of ſuch importance as this, we ſhould do our utmoſt endeavour to conquer that fickleneſs of mind which ſo ſtrongly characterizes all our extravagant deſires, but ſhews itſelf particularly in our ſcruples about religious evidence. This diſpoſition is in no caſe a proof of want, but rather proceeds from a mind rendered wanton by abundance. Overlooking the happineſs which our preſent circumſtances might furniſh us with, we think if we were in ſuch a ſituation we ſhould be compleatly happy.

In the ſame manner it happens with regard to religious evidence : many of us, I dare ſay, think that if we had been favoured with the ſame evidence which our Saviour gave the Jews in con-

firmation

firmation of his divine commiffion, it would have fatisfied us compleatly; and that the works which he did in his Father's name would have been to us an undoubted teftimony that his Father had fent him.

But the Jews, on the other hand, had their minds fo prepoffeffed with the temporal power of the Meffiah, that they fhut both their ears and eyes againft the cleareft evidence.

To ftrengthen our faith, befides all other evidence, we have the full completion of a very diftinct and particular prophecy of our Saviour concerning the obfcure beginning, and future flourifhing ftate of his kingdom againft all human probability. And by the wonderful providence of God, the very infidelity of the Jews is become a ftanding argument for the truth of that very religion which they deny.

A careful attention to the fulfilling of prophecies, and the progrefs of the Chriftian Religion, feems to be the additional evidence referved for thefe latter days, by which we are to difcover that God is ftill active in carrying on his purpofes for the redemption of the world. But as the completion of prophecies muft keep pace with the affairs of mankind, the ordinary life of an infidel, who gives no credit to any teftimony beyond his own poffible experience, will hardly upon this ground furnifh matter for a rational conviction. But if the Supreme Being would condefcend to accomplifh a few prophecies to humour him, he would believe.

In the fame manner, the Jews would not condefcend to attend to the ordinary courfe of our Saviour's miracles; but expected that he was to defcend from his dignity and character fo far as to humour every fcrupulous inquifitive fool with a

fign

sign from heaven, and then they would believe. " Nay but, father Abraham, if one rose from the " dead, they would believe." But Abraham knew too well this disposition in mankind against which I am now speaking, to think that it would have been of any use to comply with the request. " If " they believe not Moses and the prophets, neither " will they be persuaded though one rose from " the dead."

This is an alarming part of our character, as it makes our opinions so unstable, that different times of life, different circumstances, and different humours, require fresh arguments in proof of our religion. The ways of God are fixed and uniform, and are not to be suited to our capricious humours. Let us, therefore, seriously consider our condition, and not think ourselves of such importance that Heaven ought to work miracles to remove our unreasonable scruples. Let us only attend with modesty to the arguments which may be derived from the manifestations of himself which God has already condescended to give us, and we shall find them sufficient for establishing a solid and rational conviction.

THE END.